Murder Moon

A.M. Holloway

Your Publishing Company

Prologue

Four guys seated around a poker table stare at each other while another guy leans against a post. Each guy holds a hand of cards, and they study their chances of winning. "Your call, dude." Augustus prodded the guy sitting across from him to make his next move. Nothing happened.

The other guys fidgeted in their chairs while a guy leaning on the nearest post wandered off into the house. He returned with food and drinks. "Nothing's changed? Come on, man, do something. We don't have all night."

"I'm working on it. Can't you see that I'm thinking?" Tyrel asked his friends. The others sipped from a can and dipped their chips into the ranch dip as Tyrel did his thing.

Augustus leaned back in his chair, knowing he won the hand, but Tyrel refused to give in to it. Tyrel hated to lose. Augustus tried not to smile because he didn't want to give away his hand.

As the minutes pass, the others grow weary. Two guys fold, leaving Augustus and Tyrel to face off. Tyrel twirls a dread lock between his fingers as he sizes up Augustus and the cards he might be holding.

Finally, the time came. Tyrel's smile grew until it had nowhere to go on his face. He stood proudly, and he claimed to be the winner. Then Augustus stood, and at six foot four inches tall, people noticed. Tyrel backed away from the table before laying his cards down.

Augustus slapped the table and yelled, "show them cards, boy!"

Tyrel leaned over into Augustus' face and said, "you show yours if you think you won!"

Both guys stared at each other. Another guy walked over and tried to soothe the undercurrents, but it didn't work. Augustus wasn't letting go. Augustus held a straight and saw no way for Tyrel to do better. He needed the money lying in the middle of the table in a bad sort of way. It was his, and he claimed it.

Tyrel suggested laying down their cards simultaneously on the count of three. Augustus' eyes drew to mere slits. But this had to end. He nodded his agreement.

The post-leaning guy counted down from three. When he said one, pandemonium ensued. Fists flew, and cards flew along with poker chips and money. Augustus accused Tyrel of cheating. He said there was no way Tyrel had a full house.

With his size, Augustus picked Tyrel from the ground with one hand and slammed him into a tree trunk at the patio's edge. The tree shook from the impact. The other guys sucked in their breath because they knew the blow was fatal. Tyrel slid down the tree trunk and never moved another muscle.

As he stood staring at Tyrel, he came to terms with his actions. Augustus gave his friends one last glance, then he bolted from the yard, climbing over the dilapidated chain-link fence surrounding the yard and running for his life.

Under the bright moon, Augustus ran for most of the night as sirens blared in the distance. When exhaustion took over, he collapsed at the river, the same river he and Tyrel played in as kids. How could he have lost his temper like that over a stupid game? He has done nothing like this before. But something overtook him, and rage won. Could the hope of winning money cause a person to lose his senses?

The next thing Augustus saw when he opened his eyes was Sheriff Steele and Deputy Taylor standing over him with two pistols pointed at his head.

Deputy Taylor hauled Augustus to jail and then to prison after the trial. It didn't take long for the county citizens to convict Augustus of murder, and he never admitted to anyone how Tyrel's face showed itself every night in his dreams.

Chapter 1

Two years later

Deputies filed into the bullpen as our day started on this Wednesday morning as I prepared another shift change report. I turned to face the group, and nothing made me prouder than to see this group. "Good morning. I'm starting with not, so great news that you probably already know. We have a street racing problem again." I know how my team feels about street racers, so I braced myself for the onslaught of complaints.

I listened as the group moaned about the county's ongoing problem. We have many wide-open spaces and roads with long stretches of straight asphalt and dirt. So, street racing is popular. We've handled many complaints about the street racers. But, once we stop them at one location, they show up somewhere else several weeks later.

"Hold on, guys. Last night, the county sustained its first reported injury from street racing. A vehicle lost control and struck a bystander. The bystander was lucky, since they only have a few broken ribs and bruises." I shared.

Deputy Taylor asked, "I didn't hear this on the scanner last night. What time did it happen?"

"They didn't call 911. A friend drove the injured to the hospital, and from there, the hospital notified me. I interviewed Jerome Billings this morning, but with the morphine, my interview wasn't much good. So, Taylor, your first stop today is to visit Jerome. I want the car that hit him."

"Will do, Sheriff." Deputy Taylor jotted a note of the victim's name.

"That's it. Hit the streets. Stay safe." I waved the group off to start patrols.

I meandered around the office, checking on things. Dispatch was on track to surpass their calls over the last year—another budget item to consider. Then I strolled through to the jail division, where Captain Grayson ran his side to perfection. I headed back to my office with a quick stop by the coffee bar.

My desk phone rang as I entered the office. "Sheriff Steele," I answered. Then a smile came across my face as Bud shared how he missed me. With Bud and Lana on assignment in Tennessee, it has been quiet. They're returning home tomorrow, and I thought about inviting the group to my house for a cookout. Since the weather is finally breaking, an outside picnic would be fun. The guys always do the grilling while the ladies handle the rest.

"What? Have you changed your mind about the cookout? I've invited no one or bought groceries yet, so if you want me to hold off, I will." I suggested it because Bud's tone caused me concern.

Bud told me he wasn't in a sharing mood and asked if we could postpone the cookout. Of course, I obliged, but it concerned me. We ended the call, and now I wondered why Bud didn't want a cookout.

Sipping coffee always calmed me, so I enjoyed two mugs this morning after Bud's call.
Deputy Taylor poked his head into my office as I placed my empty coffee mug on the desk. "Got a second, Sheriff?"

"Sure, Taylor. Have a seat." I reached over and grabbed a notebook, just in case I needed notes.

"Sheriff, I met with Jerome. He's still in tremendous pain, with broken ribs and bruising. However, his doctor is releasing him tomorrow. He gave me a vague description of the vehicle and isn't looking to press charges. Jerome thought the guy had just lost control of his car, which wasn't intentional. Last night was the first time he attended a street race and probably his last. A guy from school told him about it."

"What was his description of the accident?" I reached up and rubbed my neck. Someone could have killed Jerome last night. I don't understand people refusing to press charges against a criminal.

Deputy Taylor continued, "Jerome stated he stood off to the side with a group of kids from school. The driver of a dark-colored sports car lost control as he made doughnuts on the pavement. The car's back end swung out too far and clipped Jerome in the chest as he was standing from tying his shoe. I expressed the possibility of death if the car had struck him in the head."

I shook my head from side to side as the realization hit me. Jerome's accident could have been a death investigation this morning, and we would have a murder on our hands. "Let's get CCTV footage from the hospital. Someone drove him to the hospital and dropped him at the emergency entrance. I want the driver."

"I hoped you would say that, Sheriff. I'll take Deputy Long with me if you're okay with it. He hasn't visited the hospital security team yet." Deputy Taylor turned and exited my office.

My head spun as I considered the ramifications of street racing. I'll ride the county roads tonight, searching for street racers. We'll find them another way if Jerome doesn't divulge the driver. I turned and watched my deputies pull away from the office.

While they were away, dispatch notified Tuttle of an auto accident on the main road in front of the diner. I glanced at the clock and grabbed my keys from the desk. There is nothing like the diner for lunch. Everything on the menu is fantastic, and it's almost lunchtime.

The traffic stopped as I turned at the light a few blocks from the diner. I couldn't see around the semi-truck I followed, so I swerved into the turn-only lane, made the next right, and drove a few back streets. I was glad when I made it to Tuttle's location from another direction. Traffic would not move for a while. The accident rattled Tuttle because he had two severely damaged vehicles and an injured pedestrian. When I walked to Tuttle, he pointed to the lady on the ground next to the traffic light, grimacing in pain.

Dispatch never mentioned a pedestrian. That tidbit of information slid to the back of my brain for later. I made it to the lady's side and kneeled beside her. "Hi, I'm Sheriff Steele. Hold on. We have an ambulance on the way." I looked at her ankle and lower leg, and there was no reason for me to ask where she hurt. The injury is apparent. So, we held hands while she concentrated on breathing.

Tuttle came over to my location when he calmed the drivers. Their injuries were minimal compared to the lady. We heard the ambulance before its arrival. Tuttle stood and met the EMS attendants. He instructed an attendant to access the pedestrian's injuries pronto.

Seconds passed when Tuttle escorted an EMS guy and a firefighter to my location. They treated the pedestrian's injuries, and she screamed when they placed her leg into a splint. Then she passed out. I jumped back when the EMS guy pushed me away. He touched her neck and leaned over to press a stethoscope to her chest. He yelled instructions to the firefighter to start chest compressions.

We stood back and watched the EMS guy do his job with gusto as he revived the pedestrian. They loaded her into the ambulance and raced from the accident scene. I looked at Tuttle, and we exhaled a breath. From there, we stepped over to the drivers and took their information for the report.

With tow trucks standing by for the debris removal, Tuttle and I left for the hospital, but glancing back, Tuttle remained in his vehicle as I pulled away.

There was no way I could eat until I heard about the pedestrian's condition. Then, I realized I didn't even have her name.

I pulled into the hospital parking lot and headed for the emergency room entrance. I noticed a man at the counter when I entered the emergency lobby. The nurse told the man about his wife being in surgery. I approached him and introduced myself.

He thanked me for staying with his wife. I asked about the surgery. "They're setting her leg and ankle now that her vitals are normal. From what I know, the cars struck her as she waited on the corner to cross the street."

"I'll leave you alone, but if you need anything. Please call this number. Deputy Tuttle will have the report ready tomorrow. It will be there when you're ready for it." I shook his hand and exited. Tuttle was walking inside as I left, so I waved at him to turn around.

We met outside in the parking lot, and I explained the pedestrian's status and her husband's arrival. Tuttle stated, "I'm going to the office to work on the report. It will be important for the lady's husband to have it."

"Sounds like a plan. See you later at the office." I walked to my car while he climbed into his. Glancing back at the hospital, I muttered a silent prayer for the lady. Then I remembered Taylor and Long had a meeting with security about the CCTV footage from last night. Since their vehicles weren't in the lot, I hope they're at the office with the video.

Driving back to the office in silence, I decided lunch would wait. The scanner didn't work so much as crackle. It made me wonder if it worked, but I didn't check it because I would find out if something was wrong when my feet crossed the sheriff's office threshold. Sometimes it's nice to hear nothing.

Maggie met me at my office door. "Sheriff, the guys are waiting for you to see the CCTV video from last night. Taylor asked that you meet them in the conference room."

"Thanks, Maggie. Anything else happening?" I watched as she shook her head no.

I stopped by the coffee bar on my way to the conference room and grabbed a snack from my desk. When I entered, the day shift deputies sat around the table. "Uh, guys, do we have anyone on patrol?" I questioned with my eyebrows bunched.

Taylor looked around the room. "No one. We wanted to see the video in hopes we recognized the car. It'll be just a minute." Taylor reached down to his laptop and clicked the mouse.

Seconds later, we stared at the emergency room entrance as the time passed on the lower right of the video screen. Just as I was about to send the troops back to the streets, a dark-colored car drove up to the hospital, stopped, and left Jerome on the ground outside the emergency room doors. My blood pressure spiked.

"The people in that car dropped off an injured person without so much as helping him inside. I can't wait to meet these people." I rubbed my temple. "Can you read the tag number? I can't tell if the car is blue or black."

"I got a partial plate, GNT. The numbers are on the far side, and from this angle, I can't read them. The vehicle looks like an older Mustang, but I can't swear by it." Tuttle offered.

Since I had heard nothing from Deputy Long, I glanced his way. By the look in his eyes, he knows something. "Braxton, do you know this car?"

"Sheriff, I think I might. In high school, a guy on the football team got a car almost identical to this one as a graduation present. I'll make a few calls because I can't remember his name, and I thought he had moved away. He wasn't on the football team when I was a junior. That's the year we won the state championship. We weren't hanging buddies or anything since I was younger. We played football on the same team for two years." Deputy Braxton Long stared at the car on the screen.

"Thanks, Deputy Long." Watching his expression, I couldn't tell if Long was telling me the whole truth. "See what you can find out for us?" I turned and walked to my office.

As I passed the 911 division, I stopped in to speak with the duty sergeant. Everybody calls her Sergeant T, since her first name is Tabitha. She's been around this sheriff's office for as long as I can remember. Tabitha never asks for a raise in pay.

Instead, she does what she loves day in and day out. Her dispatchers love her, both as a leader and a friend.

"Sergeant T, I need a word, please." I continued walking to her office, hoping she would follow. She arrived a few seconds later.

"What can I help you with, Sheriff? This doesn't feel like a social call." Sergeant T stated as she stood behind her desk.

"It's not. I responded to an accident scene this morning in front of the diner. Deputy Tuttle took the call. Upon my arrival, an injured pedestrian was lying on the sidewalk with apparent injuries. Neither Tuttle nor I knew of a pedestrian. Did the operator fail to advise us, or did the caller not report a pedestrian?"

"Sheriff, I'm not familiar with the call. Let me pull the tape, and I'll let you know." Sergeant T offered.

"Let me know the outcome as soon as possible. Thanks." When I left her, I headed to my office. In my heart, I hoped the caller didn't know of the pedestrian's condition. Otherwise, Sergeant T would have a training opportunity with a dispatcher. Knowledge of an injured person is not something we leave out of an emergency call.

By the time I returned to my office, lunch was way past due. I handled a few calls and left early. Tonight, I planned on driving around, searching for my street racers. Once I had their current location, we could devise a plan to bust their party. I would eat dinner, shower, dress in plain clothes, and take my personal car. If the drivers saw the sheriff's car, they would bolt.

I backed my personal car out of the garage at ten and headed to the county. My portable scanner lay in the passenger seat, and I listened to it squawk, but no calls came. While I was driving, I ran across an area of concern. I pulled my car to the road's side and exited. There were multiple skid marks on the road. I found a racetrack, and I stood at the starting line.

Walking down the road, I combed the area for trash or something I could use to identify one person who might have witnessed the last race. Jerome couldn't or wouldn't tell us where his accident took place. Since he was with a group of guys, he ignored his location and refused to give up his friends.

Nothing of consequence showed on my walk, and as I neared my car, the radio toned for the fire department. I climbed into the car and waited for the address. When I heard the address, I cringed. It's three houses down the street from mine. It sounded like an outdoor shed caught fire, but I wanted to ensure my neighbor was safe since she's elderly and lives alone.

With no time to spare, I sped home. The fire department beat me to the fire, but not by much. They were still laying hoses as I pulled into my garage. I ran next door to Mrs. Elderby's home. When she didn't answer the front door, I walked to the back. She stood on the patio with the lady from the other side of her home. They stared at the fire and didn't hear me approach.

"Good evening, ladies."

"Oh, Sheriff, you scared me." Mrs. Elderby stated as she drew her housecoat to her neck.

"I didn't mean to. I wanted to check on you. Everything okay?"

Both ladies nodded in acknowledgment. I didn't want to intrude on their party, so I left and returned home. Since it was close to midnight, I stayed home. Besides, I had excitement just three doors down. I watched the show from my kitchen window. It took the fire department a while to douse the flame. It made me wonder what was in the shed.

A little after one, the fire truck pulled away from the curb. I wandered to bed, still thinking about the street racers. Do they have a set schedule for their races? Do they rotate meeting places? At that moment, I realized I needed a lesson about street racing.

While the sky was still dark, my phone rang. I rolled over to answer it and glanced at the clock on my phone as I said, "Sheriff Steele." When I heard the call, I bolted from the bed, advising I was on my way.

I was out the door in five minutes with the phone to my ear. Taylor answered my call, and I explained to meet me on Ringer Road. An injured or dead person was lying in the roadway, and we needed to find them. He advised he was on his way.

We met at the intersection of Highway 3 and Ringer Road, which is a rural stretch of roadway going both ways. The Snappy Mart sits at the other end of Highway 3, while Ringer Road is sparsely populated with a few farms along the road.

"Sheriff, did the dispatcher give us a clue where the person was on Ringer Road? That's a long road." Taylor asked.

"Not really. The caller mentioned not seeing a mile marker close by, so they weren't sure. I figured we could start here and drive together." I suggested as I looked around.

"Lock it up, Sheriff. You can ride with me." Taylor instructed. He enjoyed being in control of vehicles, and I let him. We drove slowly, looking at both sides of the road using our spotlights. We came to another intersection, but we continued straight on Ringer Road without a sign of an injured person.

"I would think a person lying in the street would be easy to spot. So far, we haven't even met another vehicle. Why would someone be way out here without a vehicle?" I questioned Taylor as we searched.

Taylor sat up straighter in his seat. "What is that, Sheriff? Over in the ditch, I glimpsed something shiny."

"I didn't see it. Stop the car. I'll get out and look." I reached up to the handle after I unbuckled the seatbelt. As soon as the car stopped, I slid out. I walked over to the edge and backtracked a little to where Taylor thought he saw something. "Found it, Taylor."

Taylor removed himself from the car and made his way to my location. "What was it, Sheriff?"

I pointed to a chrome hubcap. "A hubcap. I'm unsure how long it's been here, but we'll bag and tag it. Do you have a bag in your vehicle?"

Before I finished asking, Taylor was back with an evidence bag for the hubcap. He placed it inside and slid the closure tight. We both signed the tag. Taylor stored the evidence in the back of the vehicle, and we climbed back into the car and proceeded with our search.

As we rounded a corner, we slammed on brakes as we came upon an object in the road. "Is that a body, Taylor?" I asked, with my body leaning forward in the car.

Taylor didn't answer. He left the car and walked over to the object. Before he touched it, he slid gloves into his hands. I made it to his side before he turned the body over. When I saw the condition, I gasped. The body belonged to a female. She had lost a considerable amount of skin from the right side of her body. Either something threw her into the air, and she skidded to the ground, or someone dragged her as she held on for dear life. There were missing clumps of hair from the right side of her head, and her ear sat skewed against her head. Neither eye opened when we turned her over.

We stared at each other as we rarely saw people in this condition. Finally, I called for an ambulance. Taylor went to the car, flipped on the emergency lights, and grabbed a blanket from the back.

How could anyone leave someone lying on the road so close to death? This scene caused my blood pressure to spike. Then I felt nauseous. I didn't know if it was the girl's condition or the desire to find out who did it to her. While we waited, Taylor pressed his fingers to the girl's neck. Then, leaning over, he whispered, "she has a pulse."

Chapter 2

"Are you sure, Taylor?" I asked, amazed the girl was alive.

"Yes, she's alive. While her pulse is weak, it's steady." Taylor described.

We stood by and guarded the young girl as the ambulance made its way to us. I walked over to the road's edge but found nothing of use. It didn't look like she had on enough clothes to have any identification on her. If someone dragged her, maybe her purse landed in a ditch somewhere. "Taylor, do you have spray paint in your car so we can mark her location? We'll need to search the area for her identification. Maybe she had a purse with her when the incident happened."

"I'll get the paint and mark it while we wait. She looks to be in high school, but I don't recognize her. If we don't locate her identification, we can try the school. Someone there might know her." Taylor turned and walked to his vehicle. I could hear him muttering to himself as he rummaged through his mounds of stuff. He always carried more gear than the requirement.

Taylor returned with the marking paint as the ambulance turned the corner and headed straight for us. I glanced down at the victim and prayed for her recovery. Unfortunately, there would be no speedy recovery for her, but maybe she could recover enough to function in time.

The ambulance pulled alongside my location and stopped with the back doors facing me. Taylor sprayed neon orange paint at the edge of the road on both sides to find our spot again. And then he trotted to the ambulance. Taylor knew most of the EMSs in the county, and this one was no exception.

"Mitch. Rusty. Good to see you, but not under these circumstances." Taylor nodded his head toward the victim.

"Let's see what we have, Taylor. You've stirred my curiosity." Mitch suggested.

I stepped back as the guys circled the victim, giving her a once-over. From the lack of movement, I think her condition shocked Mitch and Rusty. Rusty looked up at me. "Is this how you found her, Sheriff?"

"We received a 911 call, and Taylor and I drove out here and found her on the road. First, we turned her over to see if she was alive, and then we covered her with a blanket."

Rusty shook his head. "What happened to her?" Mitch reached over and handed Rusty an IV bag. Rusty started an IV in her right arm while Mitch took her vitals. No one answered his question.

Mitch stood as he grabbed the gurney. "She's alive. We'll get her to the hospital pronto." He rolled the gurney along the uneven pavement. They lifted the victim enough to get a sheet under her, then raised it and laid her onto the gurney. It's hard to be gentle with something that looks like it will break in half if touched.

"We're following you," I stated without question.

As they loaded her into the ambulance, we climbed into the patrol car and followed the ambulance back down Ringer Road toward town. "I wonder if someone in the county has a missing child. Or maybe they're unaware since they're asleep." I stated out loud, but more to myself than Taylor.

"Sheriff. I had that same thought. That means the sheriff's office will get a frantic call with parents searching for their daughter in the morning." Taylor looked left before he pulled out onto Highway 3. Then he glanced at the dashboard clock. It was almost seven, which was time to prepare for work and school. "It might be wise to update dispatch on the incident. The odds are her parents will find out before we get back to search."

I reached over and slid the mic from its holder. Sergeant T answered my call since she was on duty now. I gave her an update on the Ringer Road incident. She'll handle the situation from her side and call me.

Minutes later, we pulled up to the emergency room entrance. We stood back as the EMSs unloaded our victim. They wheeled her directly to the trauma area while a nurse met us in the waiting room. We shared all we knew, which wasn't much. Finally, she left us alone to join the team in Trauma One.

While we waited, I sipped hospital coffee and watched Deputy Taylor pace the room. We had the space to ourselves so that we could speak freely. "What do you think happened to her, Sheriff? I keep running ideas through my head, but they are unimaginable."

"Street racing." Taylor turned, meeting my eyes. Then I continued, "I think she was leaning out of the car, maybe to escape. When the car took off, her foot became trapped inside, and the driver kept going. She spent a fair amount of time on the ground to cause that much damage. When the muscle is visible, it's serious. I can't imagine what type of medical treatment this girl will endure over the next few months. The doctors must irrigate the injuries because of the asphalt embedded in the wounds."

Taylor stared at me. "I hadn't considered the treatment. That's awful. We need to find the person who did this to her."

An hour later, an emergency room doctor entered the waiting room. "Sheriff, Deputy Taylor. I treated your victim. Let me start by saying she's alive but has massive injuries to her right side from head to toe. In addition, she broke her left ankle. Since she's not strong enough for surgery, we placed her ankle in a soft cast. Her nurses are irrigating the muscles now for debris. She'll require multiple rounds of skin grafts if she survives. Do you have any idea who she is? Unfortunately, we found no identification on her."

"No, we're unsure of her identity. But, when we identify her, we'll send her family here. Here's my card. My cell phone number is on the back. Please call if anything changes." I shook hands with her doctor and left the building.

Once we closed the car doors, Taylor said, "it doesn't sound like the doctor expects her to recover. That must have been a horrible experience. I hope she passed out before the pain took over."

I couldn't answer because I'm appalled a person could do that to another human being. But then, just when I think I've seen it all, something else shows up that's worse than before. Taylor drives me back to my vehicle, and we continue to the sheriff's office.

Thursday is visitation this week, and it didn't disappoint. When we arrived at the sheriff's office, the parking lot held so many cars that people pulled alongside the curb, and that's a no-no. Taylor didn't hesitate. He stopped and walked over to a group of vehicles parked next to the fire lane. I watched him point to the red curb as he explained. One by one, the cars pulled away, then we continued into the back lot and parked at the door.

I met Maggie and told her of the overnight news. She couldn't believe it either. She'd let me know if anyone called about the victim. Then I stopped by the coffee bar. The aroma was delightful, as was the taste.

Several deputies sit in the bullpen waiting on an update, so I give it. A few cringed when I described the victim's injuries. I sent them on patrol with the sole intent of searching Ringer Road for anything belonging to our victim.

Taylor sat at his desk, starting on the report. I never ask him for a report. They're always in my inbox when the time comes, while some deputies weren't so dedicated. I must ask them several times for their reports. They blamed it on their dislike of paperwork.

Just as I sat at my desk with my coffee cup in hand, I heard Maggie speak with an unknown voice. Then I heard my name. I grimaced. Today had been a day already, and it wasn't even lunchtime yet.

Maggie entered my office and whispered, "Maddox Creel with the US Marshall Service is here to see you, Sheriff." I didn't answer because Maddox stood in my doorway behind Maggie. My breath caught in my throat. This man should be on a magazine cover—tall, trim, with sandy blond hair and pale blue eyes.

Until he spoke, then I changed my mind. It's obvious he expected a man to be behind the door. Maddox entered around Maggie and took over the conversation by introducing himself. He lifted a hand and said, "Maddox Creel, US Marshall."

I shook his hand without a word because he knew my name already. My neck hair bristled before the man spoke another word. "What can I do for you, Marshall?"

"Call me Maddox. Everyone does." Maddox nodded his head toward Maggie as a sign to dismiss her.

"Maggie will hear whatever you have to say, anyway. She might as well hear it from you, so it's not second hand." So she waited for his tale.

As Maddox told me of Augustus Sims' escape, I was at a loss for words. Maggie has her fingers covering her mouth. How can someone as mean as Augustus escape? Is the prison not locked down anymore?

"Hold on, Maddox. Before we go further, I need to understand what you're telling me. Augustus Sims escaped from Jackson State Prison three days ago, and you're just now telling me. Does that sound correct to you?"

Maggie knew my temper was about to blow. The sheriff's department went through hell, capturing Augustus, then the trial. We endured many death threats during the trial and protests. Once they sentenced Augustus to life, we thought the ordeal was over.

"Yes, Sheriff. That's what I'm saying. Augustus escaped using sickness as a premise for an ambulance ride. He overpowered the two ambulance attendants and the guard. Augustus didn't kill them. Just beat them unconscious. However, he killed a man and drove off in his truck the same night. We have a BOLO out for the truck, but we're unsure of his whereabouts."

"It took three days to tell me of Augustus' escape. Why so long? Deputy Taylor and I received death threats for months over this guy. What happened to protocol?" I stood and paced my office. My hands ran through my hair, causing havoc with my ponytail. I plucked the hair tie from my hand and made a new one. When Maddox didn't answer, I continued, "why after two years would he escape? Have you interrogated his visitors?"

"The prison system brought in the US Marshalls within twenty-four hours, which is protocol. The time delay gives the prison system time to recapture their escapees. Since we haven't located him, we wanted to update you and your team. We read the file on Augustus. Several of my team are at the prison now, inspecting his cell and visitor logs in person and by phone."

Glancing at a speechless Maggie, I called her name. "Maggie, get me Taylor, Tuttle, and Long. Ask them to report to the office ASAP." She didn't respond. Instead, she turned and walked out of the office, shaking her head.

I turned my focus to Maddox. "Why the ambulance ride?"

"A guard stated Augustus was in serious pain. He'd been screaming for two hours before he called for an ambulance." Maddox explained.

"Have you spoken to the guard that called the ambulance? There are a few guards at Jackson that lived here. I don't want one of them helping Augustus escape." I jotted a note on my pad.

27

"Yes. All of that is in motion. Now, back to the murder. It happened at a convenience store on Highway 19. Augustus asked the driver for the truck, and the man didn't comply, so Augustus took it anyway." Maddox stood when he heard a commotion in the hallway. He faced the doorway as the two deputies stared at him.

I motioned them inside my office. Deputy Tuttle took up his post beside me. He looked at me and knew something terrible had happened. "Is everything okay, Sheriff?" He asked.

"Guys, it looks as if we have trouble coming. Augustus Sims escaped Jackson State Prison three days ago, and no one has seen him except for the man he murdered." I explained in a curt tone as I stared at Maddox.

In unison, the guys stated, "three days." Then I looked at each one. "Yes, the Marshalls service didn't see fit to notify us immediately. They were hoping to capture him without our knowledge. He was last seen on Highway 19, and I feel sure he's heading this way." I paced as I thought through my action plan. "Where is Deputy Taylor?"

Tuttle replied, "he's on a call, Sheriff."

"Tuttle, you and Taylor will lead the investigation. Deputy Long will follow your lead. We'll meet in a little while to go over a few things. Tuttle, pull the file for Long, so he's updated on Augustus. Maddox, if you no longer need us, we need to get busy tracking our fugitive."

"Just one more thing, Sheriff. I'm staying at the hotel down the road. The conference room is available for us to use. Please share any news you have, and I'll do the same. Here's my card." Maddox nodded at the guys and me before turning and leaving my office. Just as he stepped over the threshold, he ran into Deputy Taylor.

Taylor stared at Maddox before looking into the office. "Deputy Taylor, it's okay. He's with the Marshalls Service. Come on in, and I'll explain." I offered.

"Sheriff, I know the girl's name we found this morning. Her name is Louisa Elms, and her parents are at the hospital now." I took a deep breath before replying.

"Thank goodness we have her identity. I'll go over to the hospital later. You need to hear this." Taylor stood at my desk and shared a glance with the others. He knew the tension was high.

When he said nothing, I did. I explained Maddox Creel's reason for being here, and as I finished the story, Taylor's neck reddened, and his vein pulse quickened.

"Augustus Sims escaped. How did they let this happen? They know what he can do." Taylor walked in circles as he ran his hands across his neck. "So, he was last spotted on Highway 19, and they suspect headed south. Of course, he's headed this way because he can make it to Alabama with his cousins."

Maggie walked into the office with a fresh cup of coffee for me and the file on Augustus. We keep paper files along with our computer files. When I opened the file, a picture of Augustus stared back at me. I grimaced because of all we went through to capture him for the first time.

Tuttle accepted the picture I handed him, and he tacked it to the board. After that, Augustus would stare at me while we worked on his case. Then, I decided if we caught him once, we could do it again.

"Taylor is going to the hospital with me to meet Louisa's parents. Tuttle, start on a plan. We need to follow up on Augustus' old running mates. We'll return shortly. Then we can discuss our next move. If dispatch radios for you, take the call. We will catch up later. Don't forget to look over your shoulder. Augustus could be anywhere." We exited the sheriff's department by the side door with a million thoughts running through our heads.

My first thought was Bud. It would be nice having him by my side. But then, we need to find out who did this to Louisa and capture Augustus again. On our way to the hospital, Bud called. He could hear the anxiety in my voice, so I had to tell him the latest. The escape rattled him. I heard Lana ask what was wrong in the background. When I pulled into the hospital lot, I told Bud I had to go, and we would talk when they came home. He said three hours, and they would meet us at the sheriff's office.

I chuckled because now I know what brings Bud home sooner rather than later. Just mention an escaped convict, and he comes running. But then I stopped laughing. I hope I don't have a lot of escapees in my future because looking over your shoulder is not a great way to live.

Louisa's parents sat in the waiting room outside of the ICU. They held hands as their heads rested against the wall. I introduced myself and Taylor, and they sat up in their chairs. Mr. Elms stood and shook our hands as he thanked us for coming. I asked for an update on Louisa's condition, and Mrs. Elm's started crying. I sat beside her and patted her shoulder. They explained what the doctors told me about muscle, irrigation, and skin grafts. Louisa remains in a coma. The doctors expect no changes for a few days because of the pain medication.

"Do either of you know Louisa's friends? We'll find out who did this and how it happened, but we need a place to start."

Mr. Elms did the talking. "We know there was a group of girls that hung out together. They're all from high school. We moved into this area two years ago, and Louisa met these girls soon afterward. There have been several issues, some pushing Louisa to try alcohol. We're unaware if Louisa was with these same girls." Mrs. Elms sobs as she pats her face with a tissue. She reached into her purse and handed me a piece of paper. I unfolded it and read the eleven names, passing the form to Taylor.

I turned my attention to Louisa's parents. "Is she dating anyone? If she is, we need their names too. Has she had any visitors here at the hospital?" I continued to throw questions at the duo because I needed answers. But between this issue and Augustus, my insides quivered.

After they exhausted the questions, Taylor and I climbed into the vehicle, and I placed a call to the High School Principal, Mr. Hale. He listened as I explained our situation. I emphasized I only wanted to ask the students about the accident. If no one answered, I would formally request them to meet at the sheriff's office through their parents. He agreed to the meeting, and I read off the names. He promised the students would be in his conference room when we arrived.

Taylor stayed quiet on our drive to the school. With everything happening around us, I accepted the solitude. Then Augustus popped into my head, and my mouth opened. "Taylor, do you remember the cousin's name that left those threatening notes on our vehicle during Augustus' trial? I'd like a word with him."

"His name doesn't come to me. It's in the folder on your desk. I think it starts with an O. I'll find it when we get back to the office." Taylor offered.

"That's it. Oscar. Otis. Something similar." I suggested.

"Otis. That's his cousin's name. He lived in Alabama, but his goal was to make us miserable during the trial. Which he did." Taylor said as he remembered the ordeal.

The high school sits on a gorgeous property in the county. It boasts lush green grass and shrubs around the front, with massive planters full of flowers along the front walk. I breathed deeply on my way past the flowers, taking in the scent. Finally, I opened the front door with my key, and we entered the lobby. Mr. Hale greeted us before the door closed.

Chapter 3

I reached my hand out and stated, "Mr. Hale." He shook my hand, then Taylor's.

Mr. Hale directed us to his conference room. "All but one girl is in class today. Tamara Wake has not been in class all day."

Taylor glanced at me, and I nodded. Tamara would be our first call after we leave the school. The situation made the girls nervous. We tried to calm them, but it didn't seem to work. They fidgeted in their seats and stared at their hands. Finally, Elizabeth and Marilyn spoke up, but they shared conflicting stories about who Louisa rode with that night. I shared with the group the doctors feel Louisa will survive, and if they know anything, now is the time to share.

The most interesting news tidbit was the group admitting to knowing Jerome Billings after Taylor questioned them. However, no one claimed to know Jerome's driver either.

As the conversation waned, I explained that the next step would be to visit the Sheriff's office with their parents. All eyes grew wide when they realized their problems were just beginning. Still, everyone remained quiet. We watched the group walk out the door with nothing more than the connection between Louisa and Jerome.

This situation frustrated me. How can these girls claim to be friends but run when something horrific occurs? That's not much of a friendship. I glanced at Taylor, and he worked his jaw. "Let's return to the office and regroup with Tuttle on Augustus' status. Then we need to find a contact number for Tamara Wake and why she wasn't in school today? It sure seems like a coincidence for me. We walked to the car as our shoulder radios crackled.

I turned to Taylor. "Did you understand that call? It sounded like gibberish."

"No, Sheriff. I was hoping you got it."

"Sheriff Steele to dispatch." We waited for a reply. Nothing. I repeated myself twice more. Nothing.

Taylor called for Tuttle while I considered my options. "Sheriff, our communications are down. The radios are quiet." We ran for the car. I plucked my cell phone from my pants pocket.

Taylor jumped behind the wheel. I pressed the speed dial for Maggie's cell phone. Again, nothing. This is out of character for everyone. Where could they be?

We ran through town with lights and sirens. As we entered the sheriff's office parking lot, we found everyone outside staring at each other. I glanced over at Taylor, and he pointed out the window. The bomb squad truck sat at the front door.

Tuttle greeted us as we climbed from the truck. Then Maggie ran over to us, too, visibly shaken. "Tuttle, give us the story. What happened?"

"Sergeant T received a call that a bomb was inside the sheriff's office, and everyone should evacuate. We first thought it might be a hoax to get us out of the office, but then, with Augustus on the run, we figured we needed to confirm it. So, we called for the bomb squad."

Just as Tuttle finished, my cell phone rang. "Hi, Lieutenant. Did you find anything?" I listened as the caller described three identical boxes placed around the office. They found one in dispatch, one in the lobby, and one next to Maggie's desk. I braced for the finale.

"They each contained an old-fashioned wind-up clock—the ticking kind. Nothing else was inside the boxes. You can return to your posts now." I thanked the Lieutenant and told everyone to go back inside.

Taking hold of Tuttle's arm, I stated, "I want eyes inside the sheriff's office. Pull the tapes from the last few hours. I want whoever placed those boxes inside." He nodded, and off he went.

Taylor followed me into the sheriff's office, as did Maggie. I surveyed the area on my way to my office. Everything seemed to be in its place. Now, I imagine today's charade is just the start of the Augustus shenanigans. Taylor turned to the right and entered the bullpen while Maggie and I continued.

"Sheriff. Did you learn anything from your hospital and school visits this morning?" Maggie inquired. "I feel sorry for Louisa. The pain she is experiencing must be unreal."

I shook my head from side to side. "Not really, Maggie. We walked away with a list of names, and one girl didn't show up for classes today. Taylor is locating her now. I told the students their next visit would be with their parents, hoping for information, but it failed."

Maggie chuckled. "I bet they swallowed hard when they realized they were still in hot water. Out of a list that long, you can't tell me someone doesn't know something."

"I hope so. We're letting them sleep on it tonight. Tomorrow morning, I'm calling their parents to meet in the afternoon. So, they'll have twenty-four hours to think about their answers. We'll use the conference room."

"Okay. I'll have it ready for the meeting." Maggie trotted off toward the conference room. At least I gave her something else to think about besides bombs. I sat in my chair and placed my head in my hands as I rested my elbows on the desk.

Bud and Lana popped into my mind, and I glanced at the wall clock. They should arrive shortly. I hopped up from the chair, stopping in the lady's room and then the coffee bar. On my return trip to my office, Tuttle stopped me.

"I have the video of the package arrivals. Do you have time to watch it?" Tuttle asked.

"You bet I do. I want to identify this person. The delivery person needs a trip to jail." I walked off, and Tuttle followed.

We settled in my office, and Tuttle clicked the start button for the video feed. We watched the lobby for a few minutes when a female delivery driver entered with three identical packages. She read the label on the top box, walked over to the lobby wall, and placed the box on the floor. Then she does the same for the other two. The girl doesn't seem in a hurry or worried. Instead, she acts like she's making a standard delivery. On her way out of the building, she waves at an unknown person in the parking lot.

Were the packages mailed, and how did they make it through the post office with the ticking clocks inside? "We need to find this girl. Call her delivery manager and ask for her name and number. If they refuse to give it to you, drive to their office. You can take Braxton with you."

Tuttle got up from the chair and returned to the bullpen. I watched Tuttle and Long exit the sheriff's office a few minutes later. I wanted to talk to this delivery driver.

After I sipped my tepid coffee, Taylor entered my office, waving a piece of paper. "I've got Tamara's phone number and address. How do you want to handle it, Sheriff?"

I rubbed my temple. "I'll call first. If that doesn't help, we'll drive to her house." I took the paper and laid it on my desk. I call her using the desk phone. No one answers, so I leave a message. "If she doesn't call back in fifteen minutes, we'll drive to her house."

Taylor agreed and said he had reports to write. I admitted to having paperwork too. So, I prayed for the next fifteen minutes that Tamara would return my call. She didn't. So, Taylor and I drove out to Tamara's house, which is a subdivision away from the city. Her house is beautiful, with stone and siding and a manicured lawn with supple trees. As we pulled next to the curb, I noticed no cars in the driveway. I wondered if they're the exception, and they use their garage for cars and not storage.

Taylor knocked on the door, and we waited. Just as he reached up to knock again, a petite blond-haired girl looked through the side windows. When she saw us, she paled. Taylor stepped over into her line of sight and explained our business.

Tamara backed away from the window, and we listened as the deadbolt turned. Then the door opened just enough for her face to show, "my parents are not here, and they told me not to talk to anyone without them."

I introduced myself and explained, "I understand your parents' concerns, but time is of the essence. Louisa remains in a coma, and we need to find who did this to her quickly."

Tamara looked down at her feet, then back up at me. She glanced at Taylor and opened the door for us to enter. She led us into the sitting room, right inside the door. I asked if she wanted to call her dad or mom and have them on speakerphone, but she declined. Tears formed in her eyes as she waited for the questions to start.

"Tamara, can you tell us what happened?" I asked while holding my pen and notebook.

She cleared her throat. Then she told us about Louisa's ordeal. Some girls went to a street race where Louisa saw her boyfriend hanging with an older guy. She watched him for a while. But when her boyfriend got into the passenger side of the race car, she approached him. As she leaned inside the car to talk him out of the race, someone dropped the green flag, and the driver took off. Louisa hung outside the car for a long time before the car door fully opened. She fell to the floorboard when it did, and her left foot got caught under the seat. The spectators heard her boyfriend yell at the driver to stop. He refused and continued driving down Ringer Road. Louisa eventually fell from the car, but not before her injuries occurred.

Taylor asked, "do you know the name of the driver?"

"No, I don't. I had never seen him before. As I said, he was older. Nothing has frightened me as much as this. After everyone left, I called 911 because Louisa had just laid on the road. I'm more upset about leaving her than anything. I can't sleep, eat, or think. All I see is Louisa lying in the road." Tears poured out of Tamara's eyes. Tissues wouldn't hold the moisture. She sobbed as we waited for her to regain her composure.

Finally, she looked at us. "Are you arresting me?"

"No. We're not. While what you did was wrong and a crime, we could hold you as an accomplice. What you are going through mentally is worse than anything we could do to you." I let her cry some more before I continued. "But we need help to find the driver. What is Louisa's boyfriend's name? Her parents were unaware of the boyfriend."

Tamara nodded, "I know. Louisa didn't want them to know. Her parents are protective, and this guy is somewhat loose. His name is Aidan Joseph. He lives somewhere out in the country on a farm. No one has seen or spoken to him since that night."

Taylor and I jotted Aidan's name in our books and shared a glance. "I think we have enough information, Tamara. Thank you for your honesty. This will help put the guy away that caused Louisa's injuries." We passed Tamara our cards and told her to call if she heard anything about this incident. She promised she would.

We left and walked to the car with a spring in our step. "Taylor, find this Aidan Joseph. We need him to meet us at the sheriff's office. We can criminally charge him since he was in the vehicle that caused Louisa's injuries. Maybe that knowledge will spur him to speak with us about the driver." My radio crackled, but no one said anything. I looked at Taylor as I thought, not again.

Seconds later, Bud's voice came through my radio. "FBI Agent Bud Dietrich for Sheriff Steele. Come in, please."

I grinned, and Taylor laughed. "Hi, Bud. Taylor and I are on our way back to the office." He chuckled, and the call ended.

Taylor expected to see Lana, too, so neither took our time. Instead, we hurried our return to the office. Since Bud and Lana had been away for several days, we were excited to see one another.

The side door opened as he backed into our space as if on cue. Bud stepped through it, followed by Lana, then Tuttle. I hugged Bud, as did Taylor and Lana. Tuttle stood off to the side and waited for his time.

"Did you find the delivery driver, Tuttle?" I inquired.

"Yes, I did, Sheriff. She works for a local delivery service here in the county. A black guy walked into the office and requested the boxes be delivered to the sheriff's office at a certain time. Unfortunately, she didn't know the shipper. The manager of the shipping business is pulling his security feed. He hopes it will help find the guy who mailed the packages."

"Excellent work, Tuttle. Let me know what happens with the video." I took Bud by the hand, and we walked hand in hand to my office. As soon as we crossed the threshold, Bud stopped. Since I followed him, I ran into his back.

"What in the world, Bud?" I looked around him to see why he stopped. He stood in place, staring at Augustus' picture on the board.

"Is that the escapee, Jada?" Bud turned and looked me in the eye.

"Yes, Bud. That's him. We've heard nothing about his whereabouts. But we had excitement today at the office." Bud's eyebrows shot up.

Then he said, "well, I'm all ears. Tell me what happened."

I told Bud the story of the packages with the ticking clocks tucked inside. His face reddened as he listened to the ordeal. "Is that the information Tuttle is gathering?"

"Yes. I want the person who requested the packages shipped to us. It was intentional and criminal." I stated.

"Agree. You know you have access to the FBI. We're here for you." Bud offered.

"Let's see what Tuttle finds out first. Then, if he has a picture of the shipper, we can work to identify him. Once we have a name, we'll arrest him." My desk phone rang, and I grabbed it before it rang back to Maggie. Then my blood ran cold.

Maddox explained Augustus murdered another person overnight. The victim lived two hours north of me. She was 75 years old and lived alone. Augustus stole food from her refrigerator and her older model four-door sedan, a 2010 Crown Vic. The homeowner's outside camera caught Augustus entering and exiting the house. There are no questions about who committed the deed.

Our conversation continued as we discussed our options. Additional US Marshalls will arrive in town in the morning. They'll work out of the hotel, for now, tracking Augustus.

Bud asked, "What happened now? I heard parts of the conversation but wanted to hear it all. Jada, this guy makes me nervous. He doesn't hesitate to kill."

My head bobbed as I agreed with Bud's description of Augustus. I shared the jest of my conversation with Maddox. Then Bud said, "I'm ready to meet Maddox. I want to see how they operate. He must know I'm staying by your side until this guy is behind bars." When Bud said he would be by my side, I shuddered. Knowing someone will stay on your heels during something dangerous makes accepting things easier. Now we had to find him.

"I need to follow up with Taylor and see if he found any of Augustus' friends from our last investigation. It's time to check in with them. Can you give me a minute before we head out?" I asked as I reached for my phone. Bud nodded as I called for Taylor.

"Taylor. Did you locate any of Augustus' friends?"

"I did. Two of the nine answered their cell phones, but neither admitted knowing Augustus had escaped. So, either they're lying to me, or his people didn't plan Augustus's escape." Taylor stated, and his comments spurred something in my brain.

"Why would you think they planned this escape?" I tilted my head as I contemplated his answer.

"For one, Augustus is strong, but I'm not sure he's strong enough to hinder three men simultaneously. He didn't kill them either. That alone makes me wonder. Augustus has killed everyone else that has stood in his way." Taylor explained. Maybe Taylor was right. Did someone help Augustus escape? And if so, why? There must be a reason someone would go to all this trouble.

Bud agreed with Taylor. "Augustus didn't kill the EMS guys or the guard. That seems strange. There's a reason behind it. Have you investigated the guards yet? There could be a connection between the guards and Augustus. What have you found out about the visitors?"

I answered, "we're working our way through the visitors and some friends we interrogated a few years back. Nothing shows promise yet, but we just got started." After that, I described Maddox's phone call about Augustus' last murder.

"Two hours away? And that was overnight. He should be in the county by now. But where? I'm riding by his mom's house before we go home. Lana is coming with me. Bud, can I assume you will be with Sheriff." Taylor's voice held a tinge of concern.

"Yes, Taylor. I'll be with the Sheriff. As long as we travel in pairs, we have a better chance of surviving this ordeal. Keep your eyes open. We'll talk later." Bud offered, then we ended the call. Just as I placed the phone back in the cradle, Tuttle poked his head into my office.

"Sheriff, I got the video from the shipping store. Do you want to watch it now?"

"Of course, I do. Bring your laptop over here, and we can all see it." Tuttle followed instructions and set the computer on the desk. He cued it up, and we watched for several minutes of nothing. There was no movement inside the store. No one entered or exited, and no employee was visible.

Later, the door opened with the tinkling of a bell hanging from the door handle. A young black guy wearing a ball cap entered, then turned off to the side, shielding his face from the camera. I sighed. We watched as he interacted with the employee. The girl looked at the customer several times. But without sound, we didn't know what she said. She took the packages from the guy, accepted cash for payment, then handed him a receipt. When the guy turned toward the door, we caught a glimpse.

"I've seen this guy. Was he at the trial? Let me look through the file again. We might have his picture." I searched my desk and found the file. I listened as Tuttle and Bud discussed this situation as I flipped pages. "Isn't this person in the picture the same as the one in the video?"

Chapter 4

Bud and Tuttle compared the two, and they agreed. The picture and the video contained the same people. So, I flipped the picture over. And his name is Duke Lister, a first cousin to Augustus. Now, I wanted to speak with Augustus's family members. They need to know the severity of this situation.

"Tuttle, get Braxton and pick up Duke Lister. He'll spend the night in jail if you can find him." I instructed. As I flipped through the rest of the file, I noticed how many family members this guy has in this county, plus more in southeast Alabama. His mom still lives here while his dad is in Alabama. Most guys check on their moms first, which I intended to do tonight. "Bud and I are eating supper. Then we're doing surveillance on Augustus' mom's house. I'm betting he stops in for a visit."

The guys stared back at me. Like they couldn't believe I would do it. "What? Why are you looking at me like that?" I asked.

"Shouldn't the Marshalls service do the surveillance? It's their fault Augustus isn't behind bars already." Bud made a good point, but I needed to do something. I don't want to look over my shoulder forever. This guy needs to be back where he started.

Maggie waved goodbye as she headed out the door. She turned back as she thought of something.

"Sheriff, I just heard a dispatch call for two ambulances to report to the park. Someone called in two overdoses. I just thought you would want to know."

"Two ODs. That's odd. I don't know the last time the county has had an overdose. We'll stop at the park first. Call my cell phone if you need anything." I said to Tuttle as I grabbed my keys. Bud followed because he didn't have a choice.

We sat in traffic at a traffic light and watched Tuttle and Long make a right turn, heading out to find Duke Lister. "Braxton has said little about Augustus escaping. I wonder if he knows him. He knew something about a mustang involved in street racing. Maybe this kid knows more than he's telling."

"Sounds like you need to ask him, Jada. If he knows him, he might can help find him." Bud offered, then he turned his head and stared out the window.

When we arrived at the park, the scene was surreal. Multiple ambulances, a fire truck, and a deputy filled the parking lot. One patient remained unresponsive after two Narcan shots, while the other breathed on his own. The deputy took notes and gained both individuals' names and numbers. We'll follow up with them tomorrow because we need their dealer.

After the ambulance pulled away, Bud and I left too. Our supper choice wasn't too difficult because we were in a time crunch. So, we opted for a drive-thru. I keep telling myself I need to eat better, but sometimes time doesn't allow for it.

We inhaled the food on the drive home. By the time we made it, darkness had approached. Once we changed clothes, we drove to Augustus' mom's house in my car. It's hard to watch someone from a patrol car. However, I knew the area we were going to because of the last trial, and I had the location chosen for our surveillance. We ditched the car and walked closer to the house. A knoll sat to the side and back of the house, giving us an expansive view of the property without being seen.

Every light glowed from Augustus' mom's house when we reached our spot. "Do you think he's in there already?" I asked Bud. He continued surveying the area through binoculars before he offered an answer.

"I don't think so. I've seen no movement in any of the windows since our arrival. She may expect his visit, but there's only one vehicle. Do you know if that is his mom's?"

"No. Not without running the tag, and I can't read it from here." Bud looked at me as I searched for an avenue to read the car tag.

"I'll be back. See the house to the left of our target house. I'll walk over and get the tag number. They have massive shrubs on the side of the house. We'll be fine if I don't trigger an outside alarm." Bud winked at me as he trotted off. I hated to be left behind, but I couldn't watch the house and get the tag number simultaneously.

I surveyed the house while waiting for Bud to return. Only one shadow passed by the kitchen window. This person would have been too short for Augustus. If I remember, Augustus hovered around six feet and 190 lbs. But with time in prison, I'm sure he has put on weight, and I don't mean food weight, especially with some of these guys' exercise routines in prison. He might have added twenty pounds of muscle. If so, he'll be hard to stop.

Bud walked up behind me, and if I hadn't been waiting for him, I would have screamed. He walked without a sound, and that says something in South Georgia. We have all kinds of rocks and small twigs that snap as you walk.

"Here it is, Jada." Bud reached his hand out with the tag number printed in black ink. I snickered.

"I didn't have paper, and I was lucky to have a pen in my pocket." Bud grinned. "Writing on my hand brought back school memories."

I texted the tag number to the office and had them run it for us. While we waited, we searched the area. Two cars passed the house but didn't stop. One pulled into a driveway on the next road, and the other made a food delivery to another home further into the neighborhood.

The car came back registered to Princess Sims at the same address. "We confirmed the car belongs to his mom. And while you were away, one short person walked past the kitchen window. So, I think Ms. Sims is alone in the house."

Bud nodded in agreement. "What do you say we stick it out here until one or two and then call it a night? I wonder why Maddox doesn't have a team sitting in the same house."

"I agree on the time, and I've had the same thought about Maddox," I stated as I surveyed the area again through my binoculars. Nothing happened. At midnight, the downstairs lights went out, and all that remained was a bedside light in the owner's suite. We watched the house until Ms. Sims turned the light at 1:10 AM. Then we left.

We made it home, but I had difficulty keeping my eyes open. Sleep overtook me on the drive, and I couldn't wait to slide under the covers. Today would be a long one with the parents' meeting at the sheriff's office this afternoon, and I chose not to dwell on that.

As I pulled into the garage, I noticed Bud staring at something toward the front of the house. "What is it, Bud? Is there someone out there?" I asked as I reached for my gun.

"I don't see anyone, but there's debris on the front walk that I don't remember being there when we left for Ms. Sims' house. So just to be safe, I'll walk around the house and make sure no one lurks in the shadows."

"I'm going with you." We stepped out of the vehicle in unison. I wandered to the front walk and noticed the debris Bud mentioned. Thinking back, I don't remember if it was there. I leaned over in the flower bed, and I found shoe prints. I sucked in a breath when I noticed the size. "Bud, I found shoe prints in the flower beds. Someone stood here and tried to see inside the house."

"Come on, Jada. Let's walk the perimeter, and then we can cover the prints until tomorrow. After that, we'll have the crime lab plaster the prints." He took my hand, dropping it when we reached the corner. His hand went to his gun, and I heard the gun strap unsnap. Is Bud expecting trouble? I heard nothing. We inched around the house's corner and found the neighbor's cat walking on the back deck. Smokey visits me more than his house, it seems. I exhaled when I spotted Smokey. Then I saw him limping.

I walked over to Smokey and picked him up. He's the friendliest cat of all. I couldn't see his issue in the dark, so I opened the back door, turned off the alarm, and sat Smokey in a kitchen chair. "Bud!" I yelled.

Seconds later, Bud enters. "What's wrong?"

"Look at the cat's paw. He got into a fight with a t-shirt, and we have a piece."

"That's strange. Cats rarely fight humans, right?" Bud asked with his eyebrows together. He walked over to survey the cat's injury.

I lifted Smokey's paw and found blood on two toenails. "Smokey has blood on his paw. Hold him here while I get a swab from my car."

"He must have put up a fight to have blood on him. You know that means Smokey scratched the victim, and he might help us catch a criminal." Bud walked over and rubbed the cat behind its ears while I trotted to my car.

I heard Bud talking to the cat about catching bad guys as I returned, wishing I had a recorder. That was the funniest thing I've heard in a while. I chuckled when I saw Bud and Smokey huddled together.

"Come here, big boy. Let me get the t-shirt off your nail and swab the blood." While I worked, Bud talked with Smokey. Smokey didn't seem to mind me swabbing and cutting the t-shirt off. I bagged the t-shirt remnant and placed the swab in a tube. Smokey rubbed against my pants and walked over to his cabinet. I reached in and gladly gave him a treat. Then I opened the back door, and he ran out without a glance back.

"What a night, Bud. It's time to call it." We set the alarm and headed for bed. I fell asleep as my head landed on my pillow.

The aroma of coffee spurred me to move before the alarm sounded. I padded to the kitchen, and Bud stared out the kitchen window. "What time did you get up this morning?"

"Good morning to you, too. I've been up for a while. My mind wouldn't turn off, so I gave in and got up. Breakfast is on the stove, and the coffee is hot." He kissed my cheek and walked off to his bathroom.

Breakfast was divine as I swallowed the last bite of an omelet. Then I sipped coffee until Bud returned. I tried to plan out my day in the quiet, but I didn't know where to start with so much to do between Louisa and Augustus.

"I left you some hot water this time." Bud pecked me on the cheek. I stood and stretched before walking to the bathroom. Thirty minutes later, we climbed into my patrol car and drove to the office.

When we entered my office, Maggie stood at the whiteboard, writing names on the board. "What's happening, Maggie? Who are these people?"

Maggie turned to face me. "Taylor and Tuttle suggested we contact Augustus' family and friends from the last trial. They asked me to write them on the board so they could keep track."

I heard a commotion in the hallway. We turned to see the guys entering. Braxton lifted his right hand, pointed at the board, and said, "he's dead."

"Who's dead?" I turned to view the board.

"Jeremy Luthe. He died right after the trial. If I remember, he died in a car accident over in the next county. The accident mangled the car so badly that the sheriff's office could never determine the cause."

"And you knew this, how? Are you friend with any of these people on the board?" I lifted an eyebrow as I waited for the answer.

"No, Sheriff. I'm not. Augustus was several years older than me, and so were his friends. Jeremy dated my cousin's best friend. I met him once, but the accident has always intrigued me. So, admittingly, I followed the trial, seeing you and Taylor escort Augustus into the courthouse."

"I want Jeremy's accident report. I'll make a call. Is there anyone else on the board that you know anything about?"

"No, Sheriff. Jeremy's name is the only one I recognize. I found out about the car involved in the street race. The guy from high school sold it when he got his first job in Macon. He sold it to a twenty-something-year-old. He'll try to find the bill for sale and give us a name, and he volunteered to contact his insurance carrier for the VIN. I should have that information for you in the next couple of days." Braxton explained. Then relief flooded his face as he thought I was angry at him.

"Thanks, Braxton, for the update. Lots of information there. Continue working with Tuttle on locating Duke Lister. Let me know when you find him. The team will help with the arrest." I offered as I started to my desk. The afternoon meeting with the kids and their parents loomed largely.

"I need to get started preparing for the afternoon meeting. If any of you are available, I'd like you to participate. I'm setting a meeting with Louisa's friends and their parents. They're coming to the office, and the meeting will occur in the conference room around four."

"Maggie, can you call the hospital and get an update on Louisa for me before the meeting? I want to share it with the group." I asked.

"Sure. Anything else for me right now?" Maggie questioned.

"Not at the moment. Thanks, Maggie."

I watched as everyone filed out of my office, leaving Bud and me alone. "Are you and Lana working on a case now? I don't want to take away from your jobs."

"No, Jada. We're finishing odds and ends with past cases. Even if we were, I would be here. We can work from anywhere unless the bureau sends us off somewhere." Bud replied as he rubbed my arm. "Besides, I'd take a vacation to stay here. I'm not leaving until we capture Augustus."

"Thanks, Bud. So, if you're helping with the case, can you take Smokey's evidence to the lab for me? I'll stay here and make calls this morning." I batted my eyelashes as he snickered.

"Of course, I will. Call Doc James and let him know I'm bringing it. I've only met him one time." Bud suggested.

"You got it." I reached over, picked the phone up, and dialed Doc James. When he answered, I explained my situation and Bud's help. He looked forward to seeing Bud.

With that behind me, I pulled Louisa's folder to the middle of my desk. Then, I started calling from the top of the list, working downward. Most of the parents answered and accepted the invitation to meet. I had one outstanding.

Taylor popped into my office with a concerned expression. "What now, Taylor?"

"Aidan Joseph's parents are here. They want to file a missing person report. No one has seen him since Louisa's incident." Taylor explained. It shocked us to learn Aidan's parents hadn't spoken to him. Why wait so long before coming here?

"Bring them in here, Taylor. We'll take the report." I cleared my desk, hoping the appearance would give them a sense of calm. Of which I am not.

A few minutes later, Taylor walked to my office, motioning for Mr. and Mrs. Joseph to enter first. I stood and shook their hands as Bud slid out the door for his crime lab visit. We gathered around my desk and discussed the circumstances of Aidan's disappearance. Aidan always told his parents where he would be, not necessarily who he would be with. They knew of Louisa, and when they heard of her accident, they began searching for Aidan. Last night, Mr. and Mrs. Joseph decided to come here today and file a missing person report. They fear for their son's life.

We asked questions about friends in school and outside of school. They knew of no one outside of school. Taylor asked if they had heard Aidan mention Jerome. They admitted they had met Jerome. We described Jerome's accident. That information sent Mrs. Joseph into a crying fit.

Taylor and I continued questioning the Josephs, but we learned nothing new.

Once we completed the report, Taylor escorted Aidan's parents out of the office. Then he returned, and we had no comments. Where do we start? Is this kid still alive? Did the driver kill him because of Louisa's incident? So many questions remained unanswered.

Chapter 5

Bud returned to my office after he dropped the evidence with Doc James. "Evidence rests in the hands of Doc James. His report will be ready within twenty-four hours, and then we can run them through the system. What happened to the Josephs?"

I explained the conversation with Aidan's parents and the subsequent feeling of his death. Bud raised an eyebrow when I mentioned Jerome and Aidan are friends. "I left Jerome a message. I want to discuss Aidan with him. Maybe the boys have a place they visit when they want to be alone. Aidan can't be dead, not over an accident." I shared my thoughts and pleaded with God simultaneously to save this boy.

My phone rang just as Bud was ready to comment. The caller identified himself as Jerome Billings. I leaned back in my chair as I placed his call on speakerphone, explaining to Jerome about Bud's presence. Jerome admitted to knowing Aidan but didn't know where to find him. He says he's called and texted Aidan but has received no reply.

Bud asked about the driver of the race car. Jerome went silent. I prodded by using the criminal charges for obstructing an officer during an investigation line. He bought it, saying the driver was older than him and Aidan, and he talked Aidan into getting into the car with him. Jerome can describe the guy. But the night of Louisa's accident was the first time Aidan had ever been to a street race. Aidan didn't know about my incident before he climbed into the car. Jerome hadn't spoken to him because his parents had taken his phone.

I pondered what Jerome said, then I repeated it. "You're saying Aidan was unaware of your injuries before he climbed into the car. How did you find out about Louisa's injuries?"

Silence again, then Jerome muttered, "Tamara Wake."

"Tamara called you after Louisa's accident. Why would she do that?" I asked.

"Tamara knows I'm Aidan's best friend, and if anyone could find him, I could. I've driven to every spot I know and those we've shared over several years. He wasn't at any of them. I don't know where he is. The driver of the car that night does not live in our county. He lives in the next county over and is the instigator for our street racing issues."

"When we find him, do you think you can identify him?" I questioned.

"Sure. I've seen him a few times at the street racing events, but I've never been in the car with him." Then I heard my name, glancing up, seeing US Marshal Maddox Creel standing in my doorway. "Ok, Jerome. Thanks for your help. If you hear anything else, call me." I ended the call because

Maddox had news about Augustus. His face says it all.

"Maddox. Come in." He did and flopped down in a chair. Then he unloaded.

"Augustus is in town. Someone spotted him pumping gas in a stolen car. The store clerk thought he looked familiar and checked our flyer. He called me, but Augustus vanished by the time I made it to the store."

I felt Bud's eyes on me, but I dared not look. "I guess there have been no sightings since then."

My statement didn't warrant an answer, so silence prevailed. Then, finally, Bud spoke instead. "Sheriff, explain our ordeal last night. Maddox needs to know."

Maddox raised an eyebrow and waited. I explained the shoe prints outside my house and then Smokey's fight with the perpetrator. Maddox sat up in his chair when he heard about the evidence at the crime lab.

"Smokey, the cat, had enough blood on his paw for a swab test. That's the best news I've heard in days." Maddox exclaimed.

"Don't forget we have the t-shirt. There was blood on it too. If we run into Augustus or some of his friends wearing bandages on their chest or arms, they'll be our perpetrators. I'm thankful Smokey stayed around the house. We wouldn't have the information if we had not walked the home's perimeter. Here's a picture of Smokey, before, during, and after the evidence collection." I produced my cellphone for a glimpse at the photos.

"I'll be eager to hear the results of the blood test. Hopefully, this isn't their first time on the wrong side of the law. We'll get them if they're in the system. Oh, before I forget, my team made it to town. I'd like you and your team to meet them. Do you have time today?" Maddox inquired.

"I don't see how we can fit it in today. We scheduled a meeting with the kids involved in the street racing incident and their parents. Can we meet them tomorrow?"

Maddox nodded in understanding, "tomorrow is fine. Let me know what works for you."

"Bring your team here in the morning around 8:30. We'll meet everyone then." I offered.

Maddox stood and shook hands with Bud and me. Once he left, we started working on the afternoon meeting. I needed answers that only these girls knew.

Maggie helped us prepare the room for the group. I had a few more coming than I expected. Even Tamara and her folks called and confirmed their attendance. Aidan's parents are joining the discussion, too.

I stepped aside for a few minutes and jotted questions on my pad. Some were direct, but most were just searching for information. Someone knew something that could bust this investigation wide open, and Louisa deserved it.

Then my thoughts took another turn. Augustus' whereabouts caused great concern for the county's citizens. My phone rang off the hook all afternoon with the same worry. Everyone wanted to know where he was hiding. They remembered the havoc Augustus created for our county. The jury members that convicted him are beyond petrified. I felt helpless. Like I told the callers, he would have been in custody if I knew where he was. I rubbed my neck as I wanted Augustus in custody more than anyone.

Once the room was ready, Maggie ran down the street to the bakery. I wanted the girls and their parents to feel comfortable, and what better way to do that than cookies, coffee, and soft drinks? I just hoped it worked.

As soon as the clock struck four, the office front door opened, and the girls and their parents filed inside. I greeted each person and ushered them into the conference room. Maggie had the cookies arranged on serving platters I had never seen before. I nodded my approval for her efforts.

After everyone had their snacks, the meeting began. I explained the reasoning behind the meeting, and everyone drew quiet. Maggie explained Louisa's condition remained the same, and her parents opted to remain at the hospital, which everyone understood.

I sat in a chair facing the group because I didn't want to be authoritative, even though I wore my full uniform with a gun belt. The questions started light to get a little background on the girls. How did the girls meet? Do they attend the same school? The girls started talking, but Tamara seemed to be the leader. A few of the girls answered questions, and then they looked at Tamara. So, either Tamara was the pack leader or knew something she hadn't divulged yet.

We continued our discussion for forty-five minutes. Then I asked for the car driver's description, and total silence followed. Finally, I pleaded with the girls for help, looking into each girl's eyes. "How would your parents feel if you were the one lying in a bed in critical condition?"

Each girl looked up at her parents. They nodded their heads while one mom dabbed a tissue in the corner of her eye. That one motion spurred the girls to help. They admitted to seeing the driver, but no one knew his name. He's older than the group, and they're unsure where he lives.

The car driver's description was medium height, long stringy hair, tattoos covering both arms and up to one side of his neck, Caucasian, and skinny. One girl spoke up and said the driver gave her the creeps. That was the best description ever.

Then I asked about the car. No one in the group knew the make or model of the vehicle. They described it as dark, with two doors low to the ground and loud. They provided little to go on with the car, but we would better identify him with his description.

Aidan's dad spoke up after the description of the driver. They remained quiet during the discussion, so all eyes turned to him. "We can't thank you enough for coming here today. This guy is a menace, and we must stop him. While we fear our son's life, we don't want anyone else to suffer because of this guy. One girl in ICU and our missing son are already too many. Anything you can do to help find this guy, please tell the Sheriff."

That statement stopped us in our tracks. We took a moment and let it sink in. Then I dismissed everyone. The girls gave me something to consider with the guy's description. Maggie and I cleaned the conference room. The snacks were a big hit, with only a few cookies remaining. I handed them to Maggie and asked her to put them in the bullpen. They wouldn't last two minutes.

I entered my office and found the most handsome man sitting in my chair. "Bud, I thought you left earlier."

"I did, but I came back. I wanted to be here when you finished. You did something amazing in there. The way you had them talking was incredible." Bud stood and wrapped his arms around me, and I melted. I laid my head on his shoulder while he ran his hand up and down my back. If I hadn't been standing, I could have fallen asleep. It was so relaxing.

"Good news came from the discussion. The girls gave us a description of the driver. No one knows his name, and they don't think he lives here in the county, but I can ID him now." I shared it with Bud. "I think I'll send Taylor and Long to surrounding counties to meet with their Sheriff. Maybe someone will recognize him."

"That sounds like a great idea. Now, we're going out for dinner. Do you want to stop at home for a quick change, or are you okay in uniform?" Bud asked. He knows I like to dress in civilian clothes when I can, but tonight, I'm tired. I'd rather eat than go home.

We stopped in at the local steak house. It's nothing fancy, but they always cook the food to perfection. While sitting down to eat, Deputy Taylor walks over and says hello. Holding onto his arm is Lana Nell Ivey, FBI agent, and my sister. It still feels good to say that.

"Hi, you two. Do you want to join us? We're just getting started." Instead of eating alone, we shared dinner with Taylor and Ivey. The evening shifted my attention, and I needed that. But my eyes roved around the restaurant as I searched for Augustus. Somehow, I knew he wasn't in there, but I felt someone staring at me, and I couldn't find them.

We said our goodbyes in the parking lot. Taylor and Ivey drove to Taylor's house, and Bud and I drove to mine. As soon as we left the restaurant, I shared with Bud that someone had watched us during our meal. "Did you see anyone staring at you? I noticed you looking around, but you signaled nothing was wrong." Bud explained.

"Since I couldn't spot anyone staring at us, there was no need to signal." I countered.

Bud slid behind the wheel, and I climbed into the passenger seat. With our seatbelts buckled, Bud reached over and took hold of my hand. Neither of us spoke as Bud drove us home. As we pulled into the driveway, we surveyed the surroundings. Last night's episode was too recent to forget. We walked into the house, noticing nothing disturbed. Maybe the catfight scared the perpetrator away.

Taylor wasn't so lucky. My cellphone rang ten minutes after we crossed the threshold. "Taylor, what's wrong?" I braced for whatever news he might have.

"Someone treated me just as you were last night by trampling my flowers along the front and back of the house. They also tried to pry open the back door. My surveillance camera caught the guy in the act. The only problem is I don't know him. He's a black guy wearing a ball cap pulled low. He never looked at the camera."

"Oh, Taylor. I know this involves Augustus. Bring a copy of the video with you tomorrow to the office. Then call me if anything happens tonight." I ended the call and shared Taylor and Ivey's experience upon their arrival home. Bud shook his head in disbelief.

The night provided a needed dose of sleep. I slept dream-free, which doesn't happen often. When morning came, I was ready for the day. I walked into the kitchen after the coffee aroma struck my senses.

Bud sat at the kitchen table with a pen and paper. His laptop sat open to his left as he wrote something on his pad. "You're working early this morning. Are you making this a habit?" I inquired as I strolled to the coffeepot.

"You know I sleep in bursts. I guess it's been too many years on the job. You rarely get eight hours of sleep when you work a case, and I try to get all I can. But I have something for you." Bud patted the seat beside him. "Look at the screen." He pointed, and I looked. "This guy was Augustus' cellmate in prison. They sent him to prison for drugs. Based on the internet, the cellmate was the mastermind of the drug business."

"I see where you are going with this. Do you think his cellmate helped Augustus break out of prison?" I asked.

"I'm unsure without asking him, but it would be a conversation worth having," Bud stated. "The cellmate would have the connections needed to pull off something like this. Few people can act like they are in enough pain to warrant an ambulance ride." Bud jotted the cell mate's name and prison number.

I asked Bud if he could make that call to the warden. The FBI carried more clout than I ever could. Video interviews are becoming widespread now, saving us travel time and expenses. Bud agreed to handle it right after his meeting this morning. He called the prison warden and left a message for a return call after ten this morning.

Taylor and Ivey popped into my mind as I dressed for the day. We didn't receive any calls overnight about additional issues. I texted him anyway. I used it as a reminder to bring the video to the office. He replied with a check mark.

When I returned to the kitchen, Bud had the phone to his ear. I waited to approach the table because I didn't want to interrupt him. Instead, I saw on his laptop he had Augustus Sims' mug shot on his screen. I hoped he was speaking with the warden. It would be nice to have the cellmate interrogation scheduled.

Bud grinned when the call ended. "The prison warden was polite and offered to help in any way. He feels awful about the escape. We scheduled the meeting for one this afternoon. Are you ready to head to the office? I need to borrow an office for a video meeting with a few FBI agents."

"Let's go." I grabbed my keys from the counter as I snapped my gun belt around my waist. The sunshine was bright today, and it was already warm. The weather can be a touch cooler or scorching this time of year. Today would be on the fiery side.

We reached the Sheriff's office without incident. The radio never crackled, which was odd. Neither of us complained. It was nice to chat. When we entered the office, Maggie stood at my door with a sad expression.

I walked over to her. "what's wrong?"

Maggie handed me a message. The message stated one of my OD victims from the park died overnight. I looked at Maggie and said, "I thought he'd pull through. Unfortunately, he remained in a coma last I checked with the hospital, but his doctors were optimistic. Thanks, Maggie."

Now, I have another murder on my hands. Where did the guy get the drugs? If we can find the dealer, we can charge him with murder. But will a jury convict the dealer without a witness? When I considered the question, we'll work with the surviving OD victim and see if he'll testify against the dealer.

With the recent death on my mind, I called for Deputy Taylor, Tuttle, Johnson, and Long. I asked them to meet in my office. Deputy Johnson has been away on vacation, and he's missed a ton of action. It's time he's on board.

Chapter 6

Once the group descended on my office, we brainstormed after updating Johnson. Johnson suggested using Rufus and searching the area around where we found Louisa. I explained Bud and Ivey were joining us because of the seriousness Augustus brings to the county. We'll use the FBI's resources for Aidan, too. I advised Johnson to be on standby for the search.

Deputy Taylor confirmed their appointments with investigators in surrounding counties. We're searching for the driver who maimed Louisa and might have killed Aidan, and we wanted the surrounding counties to participate in the search. Unfortunately, we only have a description of the driver and the car so far. After we finished, I excused Taylor and Long so they could start their day.

Johnson and Tuttle remained with me. We kicked around more ideas, finally running out of steam. Since Deputy Long is training with Taylor, Johnson and Tuttle will continue searching for Duke Lister.

As soon as they exited my office, in walked Sergeant T. "I have your answer on the pedestrian call." I tilted my head, trying to remember our conversation. "You know, the accident involving the pedestrian in front of the diner?"

Then it came back, "yes, I remember now. The lady with the broken ankle."

"The pedestrian was the caller, and she never mentioned being injured. Instead, she stated there was a car accident, and both drivers needed medical attention." Sergeant T shrugged her shoulders. "At least we didn't miss something that important."

"That is good to know. Thanks for the update." I excused her and tried to figure out what to do next. My choices were limitless. And every one of them was a top priority. Before I could decide, Bud poked his head into the office and said, "lunchtime." I had to check the clock because I couldn't believe it. I felt like we just got here.

I didn't question Bud. Instead, moments later, we sat in the car, trying to decide what to eat. These days decisions seem harder than usual. But when you're searching for an escaped convict, a street racer, and a drug dealer at the same time, it's hard to sort through the decisions.

Bud saw the look on my face, got behind the wheel, and drove me to the diner. I never had time to eat there after the accident the other day. So, it felt good to slide into a booth and sip sweet tea. But instead, I inhaled a hamburger and fries while Bud watched in amazement.

"I've never seen you so much." Bud expressed.

"I'm starving. Besides, I missed my lunch here a few days ago when we worked on an accident at the corner. This place has the best burgers."

Once I placed the last fry in my mouth, I sat back with my mega glass of sweet tea and watched Bud finish his club sandwich. He was a much healthy eater than I.

With lunch behind us, we headed back to the office. Bud's video meeting with Augustus's cellmate was at 1:00 pm, and we didn't want to be late. When we entered the office, Bud trailed off to the right toward the additional offices, and I continued into my office. Now that my hunger pangs no longer talked back, I dug into the cases.

If Tuttle and Johnson could find Duke Lister, he might turn on Augustus to save his hide. Then there is Augustus. He's a menace to society because he doesn't care who he hurts. After those two, we still need to find the street racing driver and then the drug dealer.

When the thought crossed my mind, something niggled. Is there a connection between the drug dealer and Augustus? This county hasn't had an OD for several years. But Augustus escapes prison, and I have one dead from an overdose within days. What are those odds? With the thought still fresh, I turned the whiteboard over and jotted down my idea on it because I wanted to remember to run it by the guys.

Next, I added the information about Johnson and Rufus joining the search for Aidan. I hope that boy's body is not in the field beside Ringer Road. If he is, we might notice bird activity and there would be no need for a search.

I realized I hadn't heard from Taylor since they left the office this morning. Sending a text seemed the quickest, and I didn't want to interrupt them if they were busy. It took a while, but Taylor called. "Sheriff, our meetings just finished. No one could give us a name, but two agencies think this guy has stayed in their jails for petty stuff and street racing. We left descriptions with the agencies, and they said they would call us if they found anything. If we haven't heard by tomorrow, I'll call back."

"Thanks, Taylor. That sounds promising anyway. Talk later." I wrote a reminder on my pad. It's hard keeping all my reminders on track. But I couldn't afford to overlook any of them. We needed all the evidence and information we could gather for these cases.

My thoughts shifted to Bud and the video meeting with Augustus' cellmate. I hope that produces information we can use to find him. Most cellmates talk, and sometimes information slips out that the other can use. I'm hoping that happens today.

Minutes later, Bud walked into my office holding a pad and pen. He sat in the chair facing my desk. "Are you ready for an update?"

I nodded, and he continued, "the cellmate goes by Tito. He claims he knew nothing of the jailbreak. Augustus talked about getting out of prison, but they all do that. No one wants to live in prison, knowing you'll never get to see the outside again. Tito mentioned that an inside friend might have helped Augustus, but he clammed up when I questioned him. He realized how interested we were in this friend, and then he requested favors."

"Do we have any idea about the identity of the inside friend? There are prison guards at Jackson that would know Augustus from school." I tilted my head and raised an eyebrow.

As soon as I jotted a note, I looked up, and Bud did the same. Then he said, "I don't have an identification yet, but I've asked for the records and backgrounds of all the guards and the warden. The warden seemed helpful, but I'd rather check him out, anyway."

"I agree. Here's the list of guards employed at the prison when Augustus first arrived. Maybe a comparison with the new ones would help." I offered, passing Bud a piece of paper with the list of names. This was the list from our original case file.

Bud answered his ringing phone. I listened to the one-sided conversation. It sounded as if the prison warden called Bud about the interview. Then my phone rang. I spent fifteen minutes telling a citizen we spend every minute of every day searching for Augustus, and no one wants him behind bars more than me.

Once our calls were over, Bud explained the warden's call. "The warden agreed to pull the videos of Augustus and his visitors. While there was no sound on his video, we could see if the visitors communicated with Augustus. Although, with the plexiglass partition, the visitor wouldn't be able to slip a note or anything to Augustus without the guards witnessing it. The communication would be verbal."

"That's interesting. A plexiglass partition separated Augustus and his visitors. Is it possible for a visitor to pass information to Augustus using sign language? Do you think they have certain words that instigate activity?" I pondered as I doodled on my pad.

The warden promised Bud the videos within forty-eight hours. I couldn't wait to see those visits. Maybe they devised a code of speaking or body movements. We had something to look forward to now.

Maddox called as Bud sat in my office pondering his conversation with the warden. I realized he never shared good news because there's always an issue. So I answered and listened as Maddox explained the situation. Someone spotted Augustus driving away from the river. They found a campsite with beer cans, food containers, and tents in their search. Maddox advised his team to watch Mrs. Sims' house while another group monitored the campground.

After Maddox concluded his statement, I asked, "Has anyone visited Mrs. Sims since you've started watching her?" I watched Bud tilt his head when he figured out who was at the end of my call.

His response satisfied my curiosity. No one has visited her, which they think is strange. Next, Maddox requested a phone record for Mrs. Sims.

He wants to see if she has received more incoming calls than usual.

Maddox ended his call when he received another call. I explained the situation with the camping site. "That would explain why no one sees Augustus in town. He only comes out at night." Bud surmised.

I stood from my chair because I needed coffee, but my ringing phone stopped me. Doc James called me to update the blood found on Smokey's paw. My mouth dropped open when he told me about the blood's owner. I dropped the phone back in its cradle and then looked at Bud. Bud's eyes pleaded with me to explain.

"Duke Lister was at the house. The blood on Smokey's paw and the t-shirt belonged to Duke Lister. He must be one of Augustus' runners. Do you have the visitation log yet? I'd like to see if Duke's name is on it." I shared while writing notes on my pad. Is Duke staying at the campsite with Augustus?

Bud explained he needed to run to his office. His computer was in there, and the warden promised to send the visitation logs to his email. While I was alone, I considered the Augustus case. Somehow, I feel the OD in the park resulted from Augustus and his druggies. If I could persuade the survivor to identify the dealer, we could pursue another murder case on Augustus.

I heard Bud and Ivey talking in the hallway. Since I never got my coffee, I walked toward the coffee bar. Agent Ivey smiled when she saw me, and then she said she wanted to help in the missing boy case. I tilted my head because Ivey remains on light duty because of her injuries from the serial killer case. "Are you sure you are ready, Lana? Don't rush it."

Ivey replies, "I need to do something. Everyone is scrambling, trying to solve so many issues. While I don't see myself ready for a gunfight with Augustus, finding Aidan is something I can tackle."

"I'll leave that up to you and Bud. Finding Aidan alive are slim, so you are most likely looking for body recovery. Do you feel comfortable with that?" I inquired.

Ivey pauses before she answers. "If we find the body, his parents get closure. And that is something every parent deserves."

"Ok. Then. Join the guys in the search for Aidan. If it becomes too much, back away. Promise me you won't push yourself." The thought of Ivey pushing herself too far scared me after her ordeal with the serial killer. I'm unsure how I would have handled it if someone kidnapped and beat me.

After our conversation, I hurried to grab a coffee since Bud was waiting in my office. I walked in, asking Bud about Ivey. He said to let her try. But, if she wanted to remain an agent, she must jump back into the fire. I shrugged my shoulders and sat in my chair.

Bud opened his email and grinned. "We have logs. I have to download them since he sent them in a zip file." Bud clicked a few keys on his laptop and sat back for the download to finish.

"Duke Lister is on the visitation log multiple times. He's a prolific visitor, sometimes more than twice a week. But then, we have Jermaine Tenner on the list, with multiple visits. Do you have any information on Jermaine?" Bud printed the list so we could mark it on it. Then he handed me a copy.

I'm puzzled by the name Jermaine Tenner. That name isn't familiar to me. Is Jermaine a friend or a cousin to Augustus? "Can we run a background on Jermain Tenner?" I asked Bud. "Jermaine is a new name to the case file."

Computer keys clicked as Bud entered the request. We waited until I heard the printer come to life. I swung around and plucked the pages from the printer. I nodded as I read the report. He has an Alabama driver's license leading me to believe he is Augustus' cousin. We have a photo of Jermaine, and I taped it to the board next to Augustus.

This is some afternoon full of surprises. Ivey wants to help with Aidan. Duke Lister was at my house, and he and Jermaine showed up on Augustus' visitation log. I needed to do one more thing before leaving for the day.

"Tuttle, can I see you and Long in my office?" I waited for a reply while Tuttle spoke with Long. I placed the phone down and heard the guys walking my way.

"Hey, guys. Have a seat. The results from the blood we recovered from Smokey's paw prove Duke Lister walked around my house and got into a fight with the neighbor's cat. Where do we stand on finding this guy?"

Deputy Long looked over at Tuttle, and Tuttle offered a reply. "Nowhere, Sheriff. We haven't located Duke yet. Everyone we speak to refuses to help us. They claim they haven't seen him for a while."

"I want you to add Jermaine Tenner to your list. Bring both guys in for questioning. Consider both armed and dangerous. If you want back up once you find them, let me know."

"Sheriff, who is Jermaine Tenner? I don't know him. Do you, Braxton?" Tuttle inquired as he plucked his notepad from his pocket.

I pulled Jermaine's background and gave them the highlights. After I printed several copies of his photo, I passed each deputy a picture of Jermaine. "My concern is Duke, Jermaine, and Augustus might stay together somewhere. The US Marshall's team has seen no one visit Mrs. Sims. So, it's unlikely Augustus is staying with his mom. But remember, all three are dangerous. Do not take chances."

Before they left, Tuttle shared more news. While searching for Duke, Tuttle heard chatter on the streets about a new drug dealer in town. No one gave Tuttle a name, but the dealer was high in the chain of command. He offers an unlimited supply of heroin and cocaine. The purchaser must buy the stuff through a small-time distributor.

Instantly, my mind wandered to the park overdose. "Taylor is interviewing the surviving overdose victim. I'll share that information with him. It would be nice to blame Augustus for the drug death, too. We could wrap this up in a neat package." After thanking the deputies for bringing it to my attention, I called Taylor.

He answered on the third ring. I shared Tuttle's news with him. "Have you met with the survivor yet?"

"No, Sheriff. I'm standing in his apartment complex parking lot now. He's looking at me through the window. I'll see what I can find out from him and call you back."

After Taylor's call ended, I took a deep breath. Today had been a whirlwind of information and emotions. But unfortunately, Aidan was still missing, which was most worrisome, along with Augustus. No one knew where or when he would pop up, which bothered me.

Bud slipped out of my office during one of my calls, so I searched for him. I found him in his office on the phone with the warden, discussing the guards. I listened for a minute and motioned Bud to see me in my office.

Sometimes listening to a one-sided conversation doesn't help you understand the situation anymore, so I opted to wait. Bud would enlighten me once he finished.

Taylor was the only remaining item on my list. So, I returned to my office and started on tomorrow's list. Maddox and his team are staking out the campsite tonight. I can't wait to hear that outcome. Duke Lister and Jermaine Tenner remain missing, as is Augustus. Next, I needed to follow up on Louisa, Aidan, and the race car driver. Finally, Taylor should hear from the other investigators about the race car driver.

My list grew daily, and as the whereabouts of these people remained a mystery, I expected my list to do nothing but grow. The multiple investigations spread my guys thin, but they're the best of the best. I have faith in seeing these investigations solved.

Bud walked into my office as I laid my pen on my desk. We discussed the search planned for Aidan tomorrow. Bud and Ivey are using the FBI helicopter to aid in the investigation. Ivey is now speaking with Aidan's parents about the search and requesting a fresh photo of Aidan. The search will start at ten in the morning. We're meeting at the edge of the enormous field next to where you found Louisa. They caught me unaware of the search, but I agreed with it and accepted the help.

Then we moved on to Augustus. The warden emailed the videos of the visits between Augustus, Duke, and Jermaine. We need to sit still long enough to watch them. I hoped the videos helped us understand the escape.

With nothing else on my schedule, I suggested supper. My body ached, and my stomach growled. I remembered lunch and knew I couldn't afford another meal like lunch, but it sure was delicious.

We exited the office, hand in hand, in search of food. Unfortunately, neither of us knew what we wanted to eat, so we drove home and threw together a grilled chicken salad with all the fixings. It hit the spot.

While cleaning the kitchen, my cell phone rang. I answered the call from Taylor. Then he told me about his interview with the overdose survivor. The survivor described the day as he and a friend walked into the park. With the weather pleasant, they wanted to exercise. So, they walked two laps around the park when a black guy wearing a ball cap approached them. The black guy acted like he knew his friend but had never seen him before. He asked if they were interested in trying a cut of heroin from a new dealer in town. His friend had used it before, but he had not. So, he didn't know what to expect.

Then Taylor mentioned a ball cap-wearing guy trying to break into his house. We discussed the possibility of it being the same person. After Taylor shared the survivor's ordeal, I knew Augustus was a part of this drug mess. At least the survivor says he'll never use drugs again. He learned the hard way, but hopefully, the memory will stay with him.

Taylor and I talked for a few more minutes without coming to any conclusions, so we called it quits for the day. I reminded him to be careful and take care of Ivey. He promised he would and chuckled.

Chapter 7

At 1:15 am, my cell phone blared. I swiped at it in my sleep-induced state, knocking it from the nightstand. It landed on the floor with a thud and continued to sound. I threw my legs over the bed and found the phone halfway under the bed.

When I answered, Maddox, didn't offer a greeting. "Sheriff. The two agents I assigned to the campsite sit in the hospital emergency room. Can you meet me there?"

"Of course. I'm on my way." I ended the call on the way to the bathroom. Bud poked his head into my room and yelled. "What's happening, Jada?" Bud asked with a tinge of concern.

"Maddox's agents assigned to the campsite are in the emergency room. He asked me to meet him there. I didn't ask what happened. I sure hope they're okay. Want to tag along?" My eyes pleaded with him, hoping he would say yes.

"I'm dressed and waiting for you." He snickered as he turned around and headed for the kitchen. I heard the coffee maker gurgle. How did he do that? He got dressed and turned the coffeemaker on before I went to the bathroom. Bud needs to teach me a few lessons.

I dressed in ten minutes and was proud of it. Bud handed me a coffee mug on the way out the door.

The sky was inky black, with twinkling stars surrounding the moon. It was breathtaking. But the closer to town, the stars dimmed.

The hospital emergency room was quiet, allowing us space to discuss the situation with Maddox. He repeated the story from his agents. Around midnight, they witnessed three black male subjects walk to the campsite using flashlights. They found no vehicle. The guys somehow entered the site opposite Ringer Road. The middle guy was the largest, and they assumed he was Augustus.

Once the guys appeared comfortable, the agents approached the site by identifying themselves as US Marshalls and instructing them to raise their arms and drop to their knees. Maddox said this was where the episode blew up. The guys looked at each other and started laughing as they ran away in three different directions.

Foot pursuit followed as the two agents stayed on the heels of the middle guy, assuming they had Augustus in their sights. As they snaked through the woods, they lost sight of the flashlights. But the agents ran deeper into the woods, jumping over fallen timbers and rock until something stopped them in their tracks.

Both agents lay on the ground, grimacing in pain. Augustus and his boys booby-trapped the area by hiding razor wire in the brush. The suspects pulled the razor taunt as the agents ran, catching the agents in the chin.

"So, both agents suffered cuts on their shins from razor wire?" I asked, trying to comprehend the situation.

"Not shin, Sheriff. Shins. It tore the shins on both agents to pieces. I'm amazed they walked out of the woods and drove themselves to the hospital. The doctors cleaned the wounds and treated them with heavy doses of antibiotics for infection. He explained those cuts are a breeding ground for bacteria." Maddox explained as he shook his head. "I never thought about booby traps. Your boy is more resourceful than I gave him credit for, but that's changed now."

Bud joined the conversations, "ouch." He stated as he rubbed his shin. "It doesn't take much effort to reach the shin bone. I bet that pain is out of this world."

I can't fathom how Augustus has the brains for booby traps. Someone is leading him, but who? It could be a friend on the outside or someone from the prison. We need to find out who Augustus spoke with while in prison, other than Duke and Jermaine. His cellmate wasn't much help since he didn't offer a name. Maybe the videos will lend an idea.

We sat back and waited for the doctor to report on the Marshalls. I ran ideas around in my head, but it's easier for me to see pictures on paper. I needed paper or my whiteboard. The best idea was the videos. There must be a reason Duke and Jermaine visited Augustus so often.

The ER doctor popped into the room as I shared my thoughts with Maddox and Bud. He stated, "both agents are in good spirits with the pain meds." Then he winked and continued, "Seems our guys were in the same cadence as both of their right shins took the brunt of the injuries. One agent might need a skin graft, but we won't know that for a few days. The guys will spend the night here and possibly another. Infection is problematic, and IV treatment is paramount to recovery. They are being moved to a room shortly." The doctor turned and left us with our mouths hanging open.

Maddox was the first to recover. "who would have thought they would have to remain here for a few cuts?" Then Maddox looked at us, and we couldn't offer an answer either.

We watched Maddox rub his neck as he paced the room. Then he returned to our corner. "Why don't you go home and sleep? I'll stay here with the guys until they get into their rooms. We'll reconvene tomorrow at your office, Sheriff."

I nodded in agreement. "Sounds good, Maddox. I'm sorry about your guys." I touched his arm as a sympathy gesture, and his eyes bore into mine.

We exited the ER and headed for the parking lot. "I want to watch the videos today. Someone is coaching Augustus. He's not savvy enough to know about booby-trapping an area."

"Sounds like a plan. Let's grab some sleep, and we'll start the videos first. Aidan's search begins at ten. I told Ivey I would be there to help." Bud explains.

"Me too. I also want to check in with Louisa's parents since I've had no updates on her condition." I looked out the passenger window as Bud drove, thinking about Louisa and her hospital stay. She could remain in the hospital for a month or more, depending on infection and surgeries. The thought sent shivers up my spine.

After a three-hour nap, we arrived in chaos at the Sheriff's office. People were everywhere. I found Maggie sitting at her desk with a line of people stretching back to the door.

"Excuse me, folks. Maggie, in my office, please." I instructed. The people in line glared at me as I stopped them in place.

"Maggie, what's going on here? Why so many people?" I inquired, clearly frustrated.

"The best I can tell is Aidan's parents have offered a $10,000 reward to whoever finds their son alive." Maggie offered, with her hands outstretched and palms up.

"You're kidding me? When did this happen? No one called me with a warning." I stated, exasperated.

Bud walked into my office with a dumbfounded expression, too. "What did I miss?"

I explained the situation with the reward, and Bud fumed. "How do Aidan's parents expect us to search for him if these people are out for money? They will get in our way of finding him. So why are the people waiting in line to see you, Maggie?"

She answers, "they came here to talk with Sheriff, but I'm next in line since she wasn't in her office. I repeated the spiel that I had no idea about a reward, and that's true. No one shared a reward with me either." I sat in my chair and scrolled for Aidan's dad's phone number. I tapped the button and waited. When he answered, I shared my displeasure with the tactic of offering a reward because all they did was create chaos. Of course, he apologized, but they didn't know what else to do under the circumstance.

After I explained the search taking place today at ten, Aidan's dad felt terrible about butting into the investigation without speaking with me first. So I suggested they meet us at the search site. He offered to renege on the reward, but the offer was out there. I wasn't sure how he planned to call it off now.

Bud helped me clear the people out of the office, but not in time to start the videos. I groaned when I realized the videos would have to wait again. We gathered our things and headed to Ringer Road. Cars lined both sides of the road, and people walked everywhere. If the reward did nothing else, it brought people out to help find Aidan. We have no evidence pointing to the field or woods, but it's the next logical place.

I pulled my vehicle behind Deputy Taylor's patrol car inside a roped-off area. TV vans arrived as if on cue. Bud's head swiveled on his neck as he took in the scene. "This is crazy, Jada. There are so many people here. We'll step over each other." Taylor and Ivey waved us over to their location. Then, Taylor suggested, "how about sending some people to the other side of the woods and have them walk in from that direction? It would lighten the load on this side."

"Great idea, Taylor. Make it happen." I grinned as relief flooded my soul. Taylor, Tuttle, Ivey, and Bud walked off toward the crowd. Tuttle volunteered to start on the other side of Ringer Road. Then I felt a hand on my arm. I looked down, and then I followed the arm to the face.

Maddox stared at me with his piercing eyes. He seemed different now. Maybe letting go of some of his arrogance helped his demeanor. "Hi, Maddox. How are your guys?"

"They're resting now. The doctors decided against closing their wounds but packed them with medicine. I'm not sure their legs will ever be the same again. The wounds look like something shredded the flesh." His eyes shared the pain he felt for his men.

"I'm so sorry, Maddox. That's awful. I can update you on the search if you want to stay at the hospital." I felt his hand slide into mine. The touch startled me, and I released his hand because it shocked me, but I never lost the gaze.

He smiled. "Thanks, Sheriff. I need to be here, and it gives me something to do. My agent replacements should arrive this afternoon. I'll update them on the situation and assign them to the campsite. Although I'm unsure if Augustus and his boys will return to it."

"I thought of that idea last night. If Augustus hasn't gone to see his mom, that might be a stop unless he knows we have eyes on her place." I heard a low rumble come from the western sky. The sound had everyone looking up at the sky.

The FBI helicopter made its arrival to a fanfare. People pointed and snapped photos with their phones. They acted as if they had never seen a helicopter, or maybe it was the FBI seal on the side. The helicopter pilot is a friend of Ivey and Bud's. He agreed to help but pointed out that the infrared camera would be useless if Aidan were dead.

Ivey still hung on to Aidan, surviving. But with me, I think he's dead, and his death came shortly after Louisa's incident. The driver didn't want a witness, and the only way to salvage that was to kill Aidan. After Ivey spoke to the pilot over the radio, the helicopter swooped low over the field and began its search. Then Ivey, Bud, and Taylor handed out maps to groups of people. The people fanned out as they followed their maps. Rufus and Johnson arrived later because Johnson wanted little people petting Rufus. It's hard for him to concentrate when he thinks it's playtime.

Deputy Johnson and Rufus met Aidan's parents standing beside their car. After Johnson introduced himself and Rufus, Aidan's mom handed Johnson one of Aidan's t-shirts to use in the search.

When Rufus saw the t-shirt exchange, his demeanor changed. He sat with his head high, and his tail stopped wagging. Rufus knew the sign of work, and he proved to be ready. Johnson tugged on his leash once, and Rufus followed on his heel.

I watched Johnson speak with Taylor, Bud, and Ivey before heading out. He worked alone on this search because of the number of volunteers. Johnson was an avid outdoorsman, and he scouted the area he wanted to search. And off they went.

My phone's clock showed me it was 10:20. I nodded as I felt good. The search started so quickly. Now, the hard part. The waiting. Maddox stepped away to take a phone call. Bud, Ivey, and Taylor returned to my spot. "With this many people, we should have our answer before lunch," I stated, hoping my statement was true because seeing the Josephs stand beside their car in anticipation was gut-wrenching.

An hour rolled around, and no news. I checked in with Tuttle, and he offered nothing. With this many people searching, I thought an hour would give us more than enough time to find Aidan if he was here. That stirred another thought. What if he isn't here? Where would we look next?

Maddox walked over and said his agents would arrive in thirty minutes, so he headed out to meet them. He wanted them updated by nightfall with an

alternative plan. "I'll call you later, Sheriff."
Maddox reached out at patted me on the forearm.

I didn't want him to go, but I couldn't explain why.
Just because he showed, interest doesn't mean I
should reciprocate. I have the man I want. Bud was
my choice, and I stood by it, but I felt the tug when
I first saw Maddox, and he did too.

Taylor brought me out of a daydream when my
shoulder radio crackled. He asked for an update, of
which I had none. Not one thing has anyone found
belonging to Aidan or Aidan's body. Taylor advised
Tuttle and Rufus are coming in from the North, so
they're walking down the center of the two search
teams. Tuttle found shoe prints, but that was all.

Two hours later, the wait continued. Finally, bud
walked over to me, "Everything okay, Jada? You
look sad."

"I guess I am, in a way. I feel so sorry for the
Josephs. With so many volunteers, I expected an
answer within the first hour. Do you know how long
it will be before the two sides meet in the middle?"
I inquired.

"Taylor seems to think another hour should do it.
It's 12:30 now. So, by 1:30, we would've searched
the entire area. I know these people are tired and
hungry. But at least the search is in the woods, and
the trees provide shade. Otherwise, the search
would have ended already." Bud leaned against the
car with me as I listened to the radio squawk.

"What do we do if we don't find Aidan here? I don't know where to look." Rubbing my neck, I pondered the situation. I enjoyed having a Plan B, and right now, I don't.

"Let's finish this search, then we can decide. There's the helicopter. They must talk with Ivey since they are hovering over the field. No one found anything there." Bud stood, watching the helicopter dip, then lift off toward the clouds.

We watched Ivey and Taylor cross the field towards us. They emerged, holding hands, looking like two people in love. I glanced at Bud and wondered if we looked like that. But, Ivey stated, "the copter saw nothing on his camera, so he returned to quarters."

"I appreciated the help," I said, then all heads turned to the woods. Rufus barked furiously. He had something. Then my radio came to life.

"Sheriff, this is Tuttle. Rufus found Aidan's body. I'm sending my coordinates to you. Notify Doc James for me. I'll wait here until you arrive." Tuttle stated with a tinge of sadness.

"You heard him. I'll notify Aidan's parents and Doc James. Also, I've sent you all the coordinates, and we need to secure the area around Tuttle." I instructed, as my insides turned to mush because I hated this part of my job.

I left the group at the staging area and wandered over to Joseph's. They knew the answer when they saw me approach. Mr. Joseph stood up while his wife sat in the car's front seat with the open door.

"I'm very sorry to tell you this, but we found Aidan. He's deceased. I have a deputy with him now, and we'll process the scene as quickly as possible." Tears welled up in my eyes as I processed the gravity of my statement. I've had to tell parents about their children's untimely death, which never comes easy. There is always a price to pay.

Mrs. Joseph tried to stand, then collapsed. Mr. Joseph grabbed her and helped her back down. Her shoulders shook as she sobbed uncontrollably. I suggested that Mr. Joseph take his wife home. Then, the medical examiner will remove Aidan from the woods and take him to his office. Then, if they need to see him, they can do so at the medical examiner's office.

Mr. and Mrs. Joseph discussed the situation and agreed they should be at home. I radioed for Deputy Long to escort the Joseph's home. The county will know the search results in minutes, and the Josephs need their privacy as they grieve for their son.

Deputy Long and the Josephs pulled away as Doc James and his crew arrived. I explained the situation, and he shook his head. "Do you have the coordinates, Sheriff? My team will retrieve the body and scour the area for evidence."

I plucked my phone from my pants pocket and sent Doc James the coordinates. Then I remembered Maggie. I notified her by text, and within a half-second, I had a yellow face with tears, which sums it up for me.

Doc James' team left with the van as they maneuvered the gurney through the field. Once we reached the wood line, I helped carry the gurney. It was impossible to roll something like that through woods and over rocks. At least I'll help carry Aidan back out.

When we walked up to the scene, it was eerily quiet. Rufus laid down beside Aidan like he understood what had happened. Tuttle stood erect, with his back to the body. I expected Aidan to be covered with debris, but someone propped him against a tree trunk. Someone shot him point-blank in the forehead. There was stippling around the entry wound.

After taking the photos, we loaded Aidan onto the gurney. When I glanced back, I said, "hold on, guys. They killed Aidan in that position. There's a bullet inside that tree. I want it." I pointed to the hole.

Bud started digging. It didn't take long before we pulled out the slug. Bud lifted it so we could inspect it. I couldn't tell the caliber, but the crime lab could. We'll wait for the results. We took more photos of the tree and the bullet hole, and then we each grabbed hold of the gurney and walked Aidan to the medical examiner's van.

Chapter 8

I prayed for his family and friends as we loaded Aidan into the van. With Aidan's death, I wondered if Jerome would share what he knew? Unfortunately, he appeared to be holding back when we last spoke with him.

Taylor slammed the back of the van closed and turned to face the group. No one offered words. We couldn't believe someone would kill a defenseless person like they did Aidan. I guess the driver thought killing Aidan was the only way to save himself.

As I looked at everyone, I asked, "Taylor, can you follow up with your contacts for the agencies you visited? I want this street racecar driver for murder. Also, I'll follow up with Jerome. Of course, it will devastate him when he hears about Aidan's death, but that might spur him to share everything he knows."

All heads bobbed in agreement. I walked toward my car, and when I looked back, everyone followed my lead. Bud slid into the passenger seat and snapped his buckle. "Have you spoken with Maddox's injured agents yet? I was wondering if they had any useful information."

"No, I haven't. With the morphine, Maddox said they weren't much help earlier. I'm hoping late this afternoon I can visit with them. I doubt they have anything to add, but I need to confirm." I explained as I looked both ways before pulling onto Ringer Road. Now, every time I pass this road, I'll remember Aidan and his senseless death, just like I remember Dad's.

I drove in silence to the office. My body didn't have the energy for small talk. We walked in through the side door and into my office. Maggie heard us and stood at my door. She had been crying, as her eyes were puffy and red-rimmed.

"Maggie, go home. Hug your kids for me." I suggested.

"I will. You have several messages from a kid, Jerome. He wouldn't give me the last name. But he said you knew him." Maggie handed me the stack. "Thanks, Sheriff."

I nodded and flipped through the message stack. Jerome's message was in the middle. I plucked it out and laid it on top. Bud watched me. "Can I bring you coffee?"

"Bud, you're amazing. You can read minds. I would like that." I grinned as Bud left my office. Why would I even consider giving him up as a mate? The quicker we find Augustus, the sooner Maddox leaves the county. That will be best for us all.

While Bud was away, I sorted my desk. My desk draws a mess. Then I sat back and reviewed the crime scene photos on my phone. I emailed them to myself so that I could start a file. When the images of the bullet hole in the tree appeared, I paused.

"What are you thinking, Jada? I see your mind working overtime." Bud asked, grinning.

"I'm looking at the bullet hole in the tree. Do you think the car driver made Aidan walk into the woods and sit against the tree before he pulled the trigger? If so, he is another menace to society, just like Augustus." I reached over, picked up the coffee mug, and took a big sip. The aroma and the warmth spilling down my throat eased the tension I felt. As I sipped my coffee, I didn't move. I didn't think. I just enjoyed the moment.

Bud waited until half my cup was gone, then he said, "your description of the scene matches my idea. The driver made Aidan walk a far piece, but I'm guessing to keep Aidan's whereabouts a secret for as long as he could."

Ivey and Taylor tapped on the door before they entered. They saw Bud and me talking and stopped. "Are we okay to enter?" Ivey inquired.

"Of course you are. I'm sorry about Aidan." I said to Ivey. It's obvious she felt the pain of the loss.

"We're all sorry. The glimmer of hope remained as long as we didn't have a body. Now, I want the guy who killed Aidan. Do you have time to discuss his case?" Ivey asked with a fierce look of determination. Her eyebrows bunched together, and her lips were straight.

Bud spoke up, "we were just discussing it. Jada and I have the same thought process as the way we found Aidan." I looked at Bud as he described the scene. He covered it from when Rufus found the boy until we discovered the bullet lodged in the tree. Then, he told Taylor and Ivey we think the car driver made Aidan walk into the woods, sit at the tree's base, and then he shot him in the head point-blank.

Everyone agreed on the crime scene. Taylor said, "I'll call my contacts and see if I turn up anyone." He turned to leave when Ivey stopped him.

"Bud and I have a call with other FBI agents about a case in Atlanta. It's another drug case coming from Louisiana. It will be an hour or two. Can you hang around until it's over?" Ivey asked Taylor.

"You bet I can. I've got a ton of paperwork anyway." Taylor leaned over and pecked her on the cheek. Then he left with Ivey in his wake.

Bud walked over to me and pecked me on the cheek too. But before I let him go, I stood for a hug. I needed one. Bud would make any woman feel secure.

I headed to the hospital with the group working on their own stuff. Maybe the US Marshalls are up for conversation. I locked my door and took the side exit. Tuttle and Rufus sit in their car, but I can't tell why, so I walk over. Rufus barks when he sees me approach.

"Deputy Tuttle, are you okay? I don't see you sit out here in your car."

"Yes, Sheriff, I'm fine. Scarlett called me when she heard the news and asked if Rufus had found the boy. I was sitting here feeling sorry for myself, but when Scarlett called, she made it okay. She said Rufus made it possible for the Josephs to get closure on their child's death. I agreed with her, and it perked me up a little, so I let Rufus eat a bone before going inside." Tuttle explained in a soft tone. While I knew he was more sensitive than most of my deputies were, but I didn't notice how much this affected him.

I looked at his SUV and saw the last of the afternoon sun. "Tuttle, go home. Enjoy the rest of your shift. I'll get someone to cover for you. If something urgent comes in, I'll call. Thanks for your help today."

"I'm okay, Sheriff. No need to go home."

"Please, Tuttle. Take the time while you can. Then, when things heat with Augustus and this racecar driver, we'll work non-stop until we capture them." I countered.

Tuttle accepted my offer. He mouthed thanks as he instructed Rufus to move to the back of the SUV. Then, he started the vehicle and pulled out of the lot.

My arrival at the hospital was expected. Maddox paced the waiting room as he spoke on the phone. He ran his hands through his hair a time or two, but when he saw me. Everything stopped. He ended his call and waved me inside the room.

Maddox met me at the door. "Hi, Sheriff. How did the search turn out?"

"Not good. Rufus, our tracking dog, found the boy in the woods. It took two-and-a-half hours. Someone shot him in the head point-blank. We recovered the bullet too. That's something, at least. How are you guys?"

"I'm sorry about the kid. But, unfortunately, there is no understanding of some people. And, yes, to answer your questions. The agents are waiting for you. Shall we?" Maddox raised his hand and ushered me through the door.

Both agents sat up in bed with grins on their faces. I started with one agent, listened to his story, moved next door, and listened to him. Both stories were identical, which I found strange. How could two people have the same story? One story should add a brief flare or something forgotten by the other.

After an hour at the hospital, I learned nothing new. The story is the same that Maddox shared with me after the incident. The doctors have not allowed the agents to walk yet and probably won't be until they remove the medicinal packs and stitch their legs. They offered to show me, but I declined the visual. Just the thought of the injuries gave me shivers.

As I said my goodbyes to the agents, Maddox asked if I could step into the waiting room again. He has the information on his agent replacements. I walked beside him to the waiting room, feeling his presence and staring at me.

When we entered the room, he took my arm and turned me to face him. I was unsure what to do, so I stared back. As soon as I saw his eyes, I knew I shouldn't have. I stepped back, but he followed.

"Maddox, please. Tell me about the agents. I need names and the nature of their assignments."

"Sheriff, can we talk about our feelings? I'm drawn to you like I've never felt before, and you are to me. We need to discuss it. Please." Maddox pleaded.

"There is no reason to, Maddox. I'm in a serious relationship with Bud." I stepped back again, and this time he stayed in place, but his eyes never left mine. His eyes held a hint of sadness.

Before Maddox responded, my radio crackled. "Sheriff Steele," I answered.

"Sheriff, someone demolished a patrol car," Taylor said in a rush.

"Come again, Taylor."

"Someone beat the car, broke all the windows and lights, slashed the tires, and wrote *guess who* on the doors." Taylor described the car's condition, and my blood raged.

"Where is the car, Taylor? Is the deputy okay?" I inquired.

"In our parking lot. The perpetrator trashed the car in our parking lot, Sheriff."

"I'm on my way." I glanced at Maddox without uttering a word and walked out of the hospital.

Feeling a presence behind me, I glanced over my shoulder. Maddox stayed on my heels. "Where are you going?" I asked Maddox in a clipped tone.

"To the sheriff's office parking lot. This is my fault. If my guys had captured Augustus, this wouldn't have happened." He reached over and grabbed my hand. "I'm sorry, Sheriff, for all this trouble. But our conversation isn't over yet." With that, he slid into his car, started it, and drove off while I stood with one foot in my car and my mouth hanging open.

After the shock of Maddox's statement, I followed him to the parking lot. People walked around, staring at the car and taking pictures. I'm sure this was on the internet long before I knew about it. Bud stood by the front of the car with Taylor and Ivey.

I couldn't believe the damage when I saw it. There wasn't a one-inch square on the vehicle that wasn't damaged. This amount of damage would have taken time and made noise. Why didn't someone hear this taking place? We could have caught the guy in action.

By everyone's actions, they knew I was mad. I didn't greet anyone or smile, and they didn't speak to me. Even Bud kept his distance. The only trusting soul was Maddox as he stayed one step behind me with one eye on Bud.

The car damage was something I didn't understand. Why do something so careless? It draws attention to Augustus, and I would think he would want the opposite in his predicament. Unless he believes we can't catch him.

"Stop, Sheriff. Staring at the car won't change anything. Is there any evidence linking this to Augustus?" Maddox asked.

"Other than his so-called signature, no, there isn't. That's the way he likes it. But we have new cameras in the office, so I'll have Grayson pull the jail yard cameras. That should give us what we need. We need to get this guy, Maddox. Make it happen." I turned and walked into the office.

Maddox relented and left. Bud, Taylor, and Ivey entered the building through the side door, with Bud entering the office and the others following. "Sheriff, what can we do?"

"Bud, if I knew that, I'd ask. But, somehow, I must control my rage. Augustus makes my blood boil. Maddox assigned another set of agents to the campsite, and I fear Augustus changed locations. I can't imagine him returning to that site again. Can you?"

Everyone's head shook from side to side. Then Taylor spoke, "Sheriff, I'm meeting one of my investigator contacts on the Aidan murder this afternoon. I'll update you when I finish." He cleared the office door, and Bud reminded us of the prison videos.

"Give me ten minutes, and I'll be ready to watch them. We can view them here. Ivey, can you help?" I asked her because I wasn't sure if I was ready to be alone with Bud. I'm unsure if he thought something was wrong between us or if the cases were getting to me. Either way, I didn't want to answer his questions. Not yet. I had to think things through first.

I called Captain Grayson for CCTV footage of the jail yard. He said to expect it shortly. Then I meandered to the coffee bar. After I retrieved the largest mug of coffee I could find, I settled into my chair and faced Bud's laptop. We had to find something in these videos. It's the only thing that makes sense.

Bud cued the video, and we watched visitors come and go. Augustus seemed to be popular. The same visitor showed multiple days in a row. "Bud, does the visitation log have the dates and times of the meetings? The first visitor looks like Duke. Can we assume the second guy is Jermaine?"

"That's my assumption. I'm marking the times the two guys show on the video so we can return to them easily. Do you see a way for them to communicate?" Bud asked.

"No." Ivey and I said in unison. But, I continued, "the only thing I've noticed is that the visitor touches his ear every so often. It might be the right once, but then he goes for the left." Bud's head swiveled to meet mine.

"That's it. They use hand gestures for signs. I think Augustus ran drugs from inside the prison, and these guys were or are his dealers. Now to figure out the code. You're observant, Jada. I kept looking at their faces, but I never could read their lips." Bud started the video from the beginning of Duke's visit. He counted the right ear touches, then the left. Bud paused the video when he saw Augustus run his finger across his lips. Why would he do that?

"Did you see that when Augustus ran his finger across his lips? That's interesting." Bud stated.

Ivey moved closer to the screen. "Augusts is talking while he is doing it too. He doesn't want anyone to read his lips. Bud, could we send this to the lab and see if someone can clean it up for us?"

"I don't see why not? I'll snip the segments with Augustus and his friends and send that potion. That would save the lab tech time." Bud placed his laptop in front of him, and he went to work.

"Can someone clean up a video enough to read the person's lips?" I asked, amazed that something existed like that. Our crime lab was at the medical examiner's office. Those guys were clever in using technology, and they both passed the state test for crime scene investigators, but I doubt they could do something like Bud mentioned.

"Sometimes they can if the computer program can detect lip movement. If it can, then it will generate words." Ivey explained.

"How long would something like that take?" I'm eager to find out what they're discussing, even though I think I know the topic. If Augustus still runs drugs, why would he break out of prison? Could he have a huge deal going down?

Bud shrugged his shoulders. "I'll ask when I send it over." He clicked keys and moved the cursor around on the screen. While he worked on that, I checked in with Captain Grayson on the video footage from the jail yard. I wanted verification Augustus caused the car damage. That would be something else to add to my list.

"Watch this at the end of Duke's visit. Augustus hands Duke a picture, and it looks hand-drawn and signed. Did we see another picture pass through to a visitor?"

"I don't recall seeing it. Zoom in on the picture, Bud. What is the subject?" I squinted my eyes as I studied a pencil sketch of a landscape. This landscaped scene showed a river flowing over rocks and all the details.

As I studied the picture, my new email alert sounded. I opened it and gawked at what I saw. "Well, well. We have three black men damaging our patrol car. Apparently, they were unaware of the camera. So, I snipped a photo of the three guys laughing as they targeted the lights on the car's roof." I chuckled as the photo printed. Then I showed it to Bud and Ivey.

"That's a nice photo. It's hard to deny their involvement when you show that photo." Ivey stated. She checked her phone for a message, but nothing was there. Ivey fidgeted in her chair.

"Are you okay, Lana? You seem nervous." I questioned.

"With Taylor investigating this killer, I still get uneasy about what can happen. My therapist says that in time, that feeling will subside. But it's been months since the killer kidnapped me." Ivey explained with her head down as it embarrassed her to have those feelings.

I walked over to her and put my hand on her shoulder. "Hey, never feel bad about worrying about someone. This profession brings that out in the best of us. What you went through was unimaginable to those that have never experienced it. Remember that." I rubbed her hair, and then I returned to my seat.

"Thanks, Jada. I don't know what I would've done without you, Bud, and Taylor as my support group." Tears welled up in Ivey's eyes just as a text message alert beeped on her phone.

"Speak of the devil. Taylor is on his way back and asks you to wait for him."

"Sure will. I hope he learned something to help us find Aidan's killer." My pulse ticked up when I thought about solving these brutal crimes. Neither Augustus nor Aidan's killer has any regard for life other than their own, and I couldn't wait to capture both.

Chapter 9

Taylor entered my office with an exaggerated swagger. That always means he has news to share. I waited while he addressed Ivey because he wanted to ensure she was okay.

"Well, what's the word, Taylor?" I asked as all eyes turned to him.

"We have an ID on the drug dealer that sold the drugs to our park victim. It's Jermaine Tenner. And my investigator contact thinks he knows someone that will spill the name of the racecar driver. The driver had a beef with a guy in a bar in his county. They arrested him, but he bonded out shortly after the arrest. Their department has an outstanding warrant on him. He skipped once bonded out, and no one has seen him since." Taylor explained with a grin.

I nodded, pleased with the information. "Is the victim willing to testify against Jermaine if it comes to that?" I questioned Taylor as I wrote notes in my notebook.

"Yes. He said he would. But he doesn't want Jermaine to know this until the trial. Jermaine scares him." Taylor offered.

"If we catch Jermaine with Augustus, we won't need his testimony. Great job, Taylor. I'm ready to eat. Do you have supper plans?" I looked at Ivey and Taylor. Neither answered, so I looked at Bud, and he shook his head. I grinned at Bud because he knew his dinner plans were with me.

"We haven't discussed dinner yet. What did you have in mind?" Ivey asked.

"Why don't you two come over to the house, and we'll grill burgers? It'll be very casual."

Both nodded their heads and left my office, hand in hand. Bud walked over and pecked me on the cheek.

"What was that for, mister?" I asked with my eyebrow raised and a glow to my cheeks.

"Because I love you, Jada. You have ten thousand things on your mind, stressed to the max, but you still make time for others. I've said it before. You're amazing." Bud showered me with accolades that I hadn't considered.

"It's hard to keep everyone happy, but I try." I rubbed Bud's forearm, and when I looked up, Maddox stood in the doorway watching me. I felt my face flush as Maddox's eyes turned dark. He tried to hide the disappointment, but I felt a shift in Bud when he saw Maddox.

Bud's head turned from Maddox to mine. Then back to Maddox. He said nothing, but there were suspicious overtones in his stare. Bud moved to the table with his laptop while Maddox approached my desk.

"Sheriff, my agents have their assignments. Here are their names and contact numbers. I'll watch Mrs. Sims' house while the agents stake out the campsite. The site remains just like Augustus left it. We hope they return tonight." Maddox laid the paper on my desk, and his fingertips brushed against mine. He looked at me, and I turned my eyes down, fearing what they'd show.

"Thanks for bringing this over. Deputy Taylor confirmed one of Augustus' running mates, Jermaine Tenner, is the drug dealer who sold the lethal drugs to our park overdose victims. The survivor agreed to testify." I shared because I felt I owed him that much.

"That's good to hear. See you two around." Maddox turned, exiting without glancing back over his shoulder.

After Maddox left, I returned a phone call from the mayor requesting an update on Augustus. I hated to make the call because I didn't have one. To make matters worse, when I ended the call, Bud stood over my desk.

"Are you ready to leave now? We need to stop by the store before Taylor and Ivey arrive." Bud stated. I glimpsed his face, and it revealed nothing. Do I mention Maddox or let it go? I have no intention of letting Bud go for Maddox, but I can't ignore the feelings either.

On the drive to the grocery store, we discussed the menu, nothing more, nothing less. There is tension between us, and neither wants to approach the subject. So, it simmered.

The night rocked on with Taylor and Ivey. We enjoyed their company whenever we had time to socialize. After we finished eating, we sat outside under the stars. The sky provided the light show until we heard a loud vehicle drive down the street in front of the house. I looked at Bud, and he saw caution.

"You don't recognize that vehicle, do you, Jada?" Bud asked as he stood from his chair.

"No, Bud, I don't. It doesn't mean the car doesn't belong on the street. It just means I've never heard it before. The car has a loud muffler. Listen, it's already driven by the house once."

Bud returned to his seat, only to jump straight up when it sounded like someone was in a gunfight in the front yard. Two of us took the right side of the house while the others took the left. I reached the front and peeked my head out around the corner.

Someone threw lit firecracker packets onto my front lawn. There were so many firecrackers the grass caught fire. Bud doused the fire with the garden hose, but not before it left a burn patch in my grass. I scanned the street looking for the culprit, as did Taylor and Ivey. We found no one suspicious. Neighbors stepped out their front doors to see what caused the noise. I waved at them and told them everything was under control.

Once that event ended, we moved our party inside. Taylor and Ivey went home early because they worried Augustus might do something similar at Taylor's house. Once they left, Bud and I cleaned the kitchen in silence.

"So, why firecrackers? Did they think firecrackers would scare us?" Bud asked.

"I'm unsure. I've been going over it in my head, but nothing makes sense. Did Augustus do that, or was it one of his groupies?" I asked. "Not that it matters. It involved him regardless."

Bud and I entered the family room and plopped down on the sofa. Bud looked over at me and asked, "do you want me to stay or leave, Jada? I saw the way Maddox looked at you today. I'm not one to stay where I'm not wanted" Bud's face carried the same serious expression it did when we found out someone kidnapped Ivey.

"Don't even think that. You're mine, and I want you to stay here. Maddox is infatuated, that's all. I told him about us, and he left it alone." I scooted over to Bud's side of the sofa and laid my head on his shoulder. He stroked my hair. We sat that way for a while until my eyes felt droopy.

He stood from the sofa. "There is no way we can stay awake long enough for a movie. Let's try to sleep. Keep your pistol handy. I don't like this firecracker stunt. Augustus is annoying me." Bud leaned over, kissed me, and pulled me in for a hug. It felt so right to be in his arms. He released me and stepped into his bathroom.

I strolled to the end of the hall and turned left into my room. What made me consider Maddox? I'd be a fool to give up, Bud. I continued into my room to ready myself for bed. After a shower, I slid between the cool sheets and fell asleep.

At 1:00 am, my cellphone blared. I answered Deputy Long's call on the second ring, advising me of another set of overdose victims. This set is in the bar parking lot on the county's edge. I slid my legs from the bed and looked up to see Bud standing in the doorway. After explaining the situation, we dressed and met in the kitchen. Bud handed me a large mug of steaming hot coffee. I grinned.

He slid behind the wheel, and we left to visit yet another overdose scene. On arrival, Deputy Long showed the victim's location. They sat propped against the side of the building facing the woods. The busboy found them when he came outside for a smoke break.

A needle remained in the girl victim's arm while the boy's head fell forward with his chin resting on his chest. These two were young, just like the others from the park. I stepped away from the bodies when I heard Doc James speaking with Bud.

"Doc. Can you run the drugs to the crime lab? I want to know the contents of that syringe." I stated.

"Sure will, Sheriff. Do you think we have a cocktail here? That would explain why the deaths occurred so soon after the needle prick." Doc James surmised.

"Thanks, Doc. I'll stop by later to see what you found." I joined Bud and Long beside our car. Long spoke with the bar patrons, but no one fessed up to seeing the drug deal. But he gave us some good news when he mentioned someone spotted Duke Lister inside the bar earlier in the evening after Long passed around Duke's picture. But, again, no one confirmed Augustus and Jermaine in the bar.

Are the three guys still running together, or have they split? I see no reason for them to separate. Augustus was the leader, so Duke and Jermaine would never break from him. Now, I wonder if the guys went back to the river campsite. While we were standing beside my car, my cellphone rang.

I answered the call from Taylor. He heard about the deaths over the scanner and asked if he needed to respond. It makes my heart happy to have my guys on my team. They always look out for me. I shared information about the scene and suggested he go back to sleep. He chuckled and ended the call.

As we prepared to leave, I invited Deputy Long to meet me at the medical examiner's office around 9:00 am. Doc James will let us know what type of drugs are in the victims' system.

With the scene secure, Bud and I returned home to grab sleep while we could. Unfortunately, my body suffers from a lack of sleep and working on multiple investigations. I'm irritable that we haven't captured Augustus yet, or Aidan's killer, and I see no end to either.

Three hours later, I sat in my office with Bud, responding to emails on his laptop. He and Ivey continued to help with FBI duties, but since Ivey's encounter with a killer, they've been staying close to home. Since they have a video conference this morning, I'm heading to the medical examiner's office to meet Deputy Long. We needed to dig deeper into these drug overdose deaths.

I glanced at my clock and realized I hadn't heard from Maddox. Maybe I should assume the trio didn't stay at the campsite last night. Otherwise, he would've called.

Since it was almost time to meet Doc James, I kissed Bud on the cheek and headed out the door. I cruised around the town, passing my dad's memory plaque, then continued to Doc James' office. Something had me feeling uneasy, but I couldn't pinpoint the reason.

As I parked my car, Maddox called. I was correct in assuming that the trio never showed at the campsite. He agreed to watch the site again tonight, and there have been no attempts to speak with Mrs. Sims. Maddox called a lab tech from the US Marshalls office, and she has agreed to try CCTV footage from cameras in town.

I explained how few of our businesses or intersections have traffic cameras. He understood, and they'll work with what was available. Maddox emphasized they were not leaving until Augustus was behind bars.

After I ended the call, I felt a shiver creep up my spine. Is someone watching me? I surveyed the area and saw no one was suspicious. Deputy Long hadn't arrived yet, but I could meet with Doc James until he shows.

I scanned the surrounding lot as I made my way into the building. Just as I was about to face the door, I felt a presence, so I turned and reached for my weapon. Unfortunately, my gun never left its holster, and everything went dark before my body hit the ground.

Deputies Long and Tuttle walked toward the medical examiner's office side by side, talking about life. Tuttle occasionally stopped by to see Scarlett, who volunteered to help at the medical examiner's office. She's an exceptional nurse, achieving RN at an early age. Tuttle and Scarlett talked about their future together, but they've made no plans yet.

"What is that?" Long asked Tuttle as he pointed to the area by the door.

Tuttle ran to the Sheriff's side and gently turned her onto her back. "Call it in, Long. I'll call Scarlett to come out here."

Both guys handled their objectives, then they waited. Scarlett was the first person on the scene, carrying a medical bag. It frightened Scarlett to see the Sheriff lying on the ground unconscious.

Scarlett went to work checking the Sheriff's vital signs. All were good, but there was a nasty gash on the Sheriff's right temple. Scarlett cleaned it the best she could with what she had, but the Sheriff needed to be in a trauma room as the gash pumped blood onto the sidewalk.

"Can someone check on the ambulance? Sheriff Steele needs to be in a trauma room. Her gash is nasty. She responded to pain stimuli, but she should be awake by now. Unfortunately, this bag doesn't have smelling salts, either." Scarlett continued to address Sheriff Steele's injuries. She has a scraped elbow from where she hit the sidewalk, and blood continued to flow from the head wound even with the compress.

Long stated, "ETA two minutes." Just as Long ended his commentary, they heard screeching tires before the cars were visible. Long, Tuttle and Scarlett watched as Bud pulled up to the scene, followed by Taylor and Ivey.

Bud barked orders, but when he saw Tuttle shaking his head, he stopped. Tuttle explained, "Scarlett checked her vitals, and they're good. An ambulance is due in a moment. No one saw anything. Long and I walked up to the medical examiner's door and found her laying on the sidewalk with her feet in the grass."

Taylor added, "someone jumped her before she could make it to the door." He surveyed the area, finding a hidden camera in the dogwood tree.

Then Tuttle said, "I forgot to show you this. It was lying on her body when we arrived."

Taylor, Bud, and Ivey read the note. It has Guess Who printed in black marker. It was all the deputies could do to control Bud. "How could Augustus or one of his guys get this close to Jada without her knowing? I can't believe this." Bud stood, paced, and ran his fingers through his hair.

All Ivey said was, "solo trips end today. For everyone."

The ambulance attendants walked over to the Sheriff and pointed at her. "Is that Sheriff Steele? Move it, guys. We have no time to waste."

Once they realized Sheriff Steele was the victim, they operated at a much faster pace. Bud rode in the ambulance while the others followed, including Scarlett. She was first on the scene and wanted to be part of the treatment team.

Arrival in the emergency room was spectacular. Doctors and nurses lined the entrance waiting for their chance to see the Sheriff. Blood continued to drain onto the pillow even though Scarlett wrapped gauze around the wound.

One doctor, obviously in the lead, shouted orders through the chaos. Nurses and techs prepared tests, drew blood, and called for a CT scan of her head. While this ensued, Bud and the group stayed in the waiting room.

There was no way he could sit still, so he walked. He couldn't count the cups of coffee he swallowed before hearing the news.

Jada's doctor appeared in the waiting room and said, "Sheriff Steele remains unconscious. The gash on her head remains open because of swelling. Once it diminishes, we'll stitch it. She has no broken bones. So, in reality, she got out lucky because her injuries could be much worse. We'll stay in touch."

Tuttle and Taylor exchanged glances and exhaled a breath they didn't know they held. Taylor will take over the day-to-day duties at the sheriff's office while the sheriff recovers. Taylor walked over to Bud and Ivey, talking about the situation. Bud and Ivey will stay at the hospital while Taylor and Tuttle return to the Sheriff's Office. Long worked the night shift, so he needed to go home to rest.

As soon as the guys left the waiting room, Maddox rushed in with his jacket flapping behind him. He stopped short when he saw Bud and Ivey. Ivey excused herself, leaving Maddox with Bud. Neither man wanted to talk first, but the situation was more than Maddox could handle. "How is she, Bud? Please tell me she'll survive."

Bud didn't go easy on him. "We're praying for the best. But, unfortunately, she's still unconscious."

Maddox paced and rubbed his neck. "I can't believe this guy. What kind of person would attack the Sheriff? And the attack was in broad daylight."

"He has nothing to lose, Maddox. Augustus is a prison escapee. He knows the likelihood of him surviving this is nil. But I can't figure out his reason for doing it. Something triggered the escape. Have you looked at that angle?" Bud asked.

"We've investigated everything. The prison guards seem to be okay, but we have one guard on vacation." Maddox looked at Bud.

Chapter 10

Bud raised his eyebrow. "That doesn't strike you as odd?" Bud rubbed his forehead as frustration eased into his soul. "Maddox, get your mind off Sheriff Steele and onto the job you came to oversee. The guard on vacation should have been your number one target."

With wide eyes, Maddox looked at Bud. "You're right. That changes now. The US Marshalls sent me down here because I'm the best at fugitive recovery. Although, I'll admit Sheriff Steele caught me by surprise."

"She did me too. I was just lucky enough to get to her first." Bud winked at Maddox. "We'll stay in touch. I'm working from here. Deputy Taylor is in charge of the Sheriff's Office while the Sheriff is out. So, stay in contact with us. We have a job, which doesn't stop because of what happened to Sheriff Steele."

"I understand." Maddox leaned over and shook Bud's hand. Then he left without another word. Maddox couldn't bring himself to tell Bud how bad he felt about the Sheriff's injury. It's his fault. If he had done his job, Augustus would be behind bars now. He glanced back over his shoulder, looking at the hospital. In a whisper, Maddox promised Sheriff Steele he would capture Augustus.

Ivey returned to the waiting room to find Bud sitting alone. She walked over and took the seat beside him. They remained quiet for a while, and then Bud recounted the time the team stayed in this same hospital waiting room for her. Ivey glanced at him with raised eyebrows.

"That was hard, Ivey. When the doctors told us about the brain bleed, we thought we had lost you. It was miserable not knowing what would happen. Taylor stayed in your room while we camped out here." Bud shared his feelings on Ivey's ordeal for the first time since it happened.

"Bud, I never knew that. All I remember seeing when I awoke was Taylor, but everything was hazy. I still see bits and pieces of memories, but that's it. I can still hear Jada tell me you all caught the bad guys. After I heard that, I felt I could finally relax. The memories stopped coming about two weeks ago. I'm sleeping better now. I feel stronger and ready to take cases again, but not until Jada is better and someone apprehends Augustus and his crew."

Bud nodded in agreement and said, "we aren't changing anything right now. Augustus is the top priority. I spoke with Maddox about his tactics. His focus is now on a prison guard who went on vacation a day before the escape."

Ivey's head turned to meet Bud's. "Are you kidding? He hasn't checked the guards out yet. What has he been doing this whole time?" Ivey asked as her blood pressure spiked.

With a chuckle, Bud replied, "trying to steal my girl."

After Bud's statement sunk in, Ivey laughed. She couldn't help it. It just came out. "There is no way Jada is giving you up for that arrogant man."

"I hope you're right, but I sent him packing. I told him to do his job before one of us gets killed. He now has three people on his team injured." Bud explained.

Ivey nodded as she considered Bud's statement about Jada and Maddox. She noticed how those two looked at each other, but she never thought Jada would have given up on Bud. The attraction between others always happens, but it doesn't mean you leave your partner for them.

Bud stepped over to the coffee bar and made two cups. He handed one to Ivey, and they settled in for the wait. The mayor stopped by, as did several council people, but they didn't stay long. Bud grabbed a power nap when he could. Ivey didn't because she never gained the ability to take power naps.

Shortly after noon, Taylor calls Ivey. He checked on the Sheriff's condition. Then he explained his call. Ivey asks Taylor to hold because she wants Bud to hear this too. She placed the phone on speakerphone. "Go ahead. We're both here." Ivey said.

"Sal, from the Snappy Mart, called for Sheriff Steele. I had to explain the circumstances why I was acting Sheriff. He finally agreed to speak with Tuttle and me. We're on our way to see him now. He says he'll only meet in person." Taylor explained.

"Call us back when you speak with Sal. This sounds promising." Bud said.

Ivey and Taylor spoke again before ending the call. Then Ivey and Bud leaned back in their chairs, wondering what Sal had to say to the guys. Could he have seen Augustus, or maybe he knows who killed Aidan?

Taylor and Tuttle arrived at Sal's, finding him standing at the door. Sal greeted them and then ushered them into his office, closing the door as the deputies shared a glance. "Thanks for coming. I sure was sorry to hear about the Sheriff. I pray she'll be okay."

"She's holding her own, Sal. What do you want to discuss?" Taylor prodded Sal to move ahead.

"It's not what I want to discuss. It's what I want to show you, fellows." Sal sat in his chair, cued the video, and then turned the laptop to face the deputies.

They watched in silence until a van pulled alongside the gas pumps. A black guy gets out of the sliding door, keeping his head down until he leans in to remove the nozzle from the pump. Taylor says, "that's Augustus."

"You're right. I wanted you to see him. That means he's still in the area. He drove away without paying. Of course, that's why I looked at the overnight video. My employee didn't recognize Augustus, but I did. I have a partial tag number too. Here it is. Find this guy. He's the meanest person I've ever met. I thought he would simmer down when he got married, but that didn't happen."

Taylor looked at Tuttle, then in unison, "he's married? No one ever mentioned that."

"He married right out of high school when he thought he would play pro ball. They moved away. He was visiting when he murdered Tyrel." Sal shared information that neither Taylor nor Tuttle knew.

Taylor and Tuttle stood and shook hands with Sal. They thanked him for the information and would pass it along to the US Marshall overseeing Augustus' capture. Then Sal said he emailed the video to Sheriff Steele before he knew of her incident.

When the guys returned to their car, they called Ivey and repeated their conversation with Sal. Taylor advised he'll run the tag as soon as they end the call. Everyone knows it's a stolen vehicle, but from where? Bud suggested the guys notify Maddox of the unfamiliar vehicle and the new area of the county where Sal spotted them.

Tuttle looked over at Taylor. "I heard no one mention Augustus married right out of high school. Wonder who he married?"

"I agree. That bit of information never surfaced during the trial. Wonder why he hasn't attempted contact with her? Or maybe he has, and we don't know it. If she were out of town, their contact would be by phone. Strangely, he would come here instead of his wife's location." Taylor said, then he contemplated his questions.

The rest of the car ride was silent except for the radio. Dispatch toned for an ambulance, along with the fire department, to the plant in town. Unfortunately, someone has their arm stuck in a piece of machinery. The guys groaned when they felt the pain of the plant worker.

Taylor entered the office and ran the tag for the gold van. The county has only one gold Toyota van registered in this county, and it belongs to an older lady, Hazel Poller. Tuttle doesn't like the sound of this and suggests he and Taylor do a welfare check on the van's owner.

They returned to Tuttle's car, driving to the house in town. The van owner's home sits on a side street in the city. The house is three down from the street's corner. Tuttle parked the car at the curb, and they approached with caution. Both guys have their hands on their guns. What if Augustus has taken up residence in the lady's house?

With the blinds closed, they see nothing through the front windows. So, they walked around to the back. Each window blind is closed, affording no visual. Just as Taylor was going to suggest they leave, he glimpsed someone's foot. "Tuttle, look in the crack in the blind and tell me if that looks like a foot on the floor. I can't see the body because of the kitchen counter."

Tuttle looked, "it does. The foot has a bedroom shoe on it, just like my mom wears."

Taylor walked around to the carport door, broke the windowpane closest to the doorknob, reached in, turned the knob and deadbolt, letting them inside. The odor was unmistakable. They had no reason to check for life, so Taylor called Doc James.

While they waited for Doc James to arrive, they searched the area for any evidence. They opted for the outside search first. They found no outdoor security cameras, but they got lucky when they went inside. As a precaution against the odor, they covered their mouths and noses with a mask. Once inside, they discovered someone stepped in blood and left a perfect shoe print. The shoe print would add to their growing list of evidence.

Doc James arrived just as the guys found the print. Taylor motioned for the lab techs to enter the house since they had begun their search. The deputies listened as the techs snapped photos while discussing various topics. Taylor and Tuttle found nothing else disturbed in the house.

The guys returned to the kitchen and witnessed Doc James pull the thermometer from the victim's liver. "She's been dead at least forty-eight hours. The victim shows no sign of a fight. It's like the killer entered the house, killed her, and left. We have no way of knowing if she knew Augustus. Maybe a neighbor knows this lady."

"We'll start canvassing the area now, but I've noticed no neighbors checking out the activity. We'll be in touch, Doc," Taylor stated.

"Hey guys, how's the Sheriff? I heard she took a nasty bump on the head at my office door?" Doc James asked.

Taylor looked at Tuttle, and Tuttle answered, "she did. Deputy Long and I found her. She remains unconscious, but the doctors are optimistic about her full recovery."

Doc James nodded. "I sure hope so. I've requested the county to add security cameras to my door. We'll see how long they take to approve the requisition."

Both deputies nodded their approval as a lab tech walked up to their group. While the tech spoke with Doc James, Taylor and Tuttle slipped away. They walked to the next-door neighbor on the right. The doorbell chimed, but no one responded. Taylor slid a card into the crack between the frame and the door.

The guys continued down the street with little luck until they reached the next to the last house on the road. They heard the doorknob turn, then a series of deadbolts, and when she opened the door, a chain remained in place—a sweet older lady with snow-white hair peered at them.

Taylor introduced them to Mrs. Canton, and after a few seconds of delay, she agreed to let them come inside. They entered a small foyer, and she ushered them into a formal living room. The furniture is pristine and probably dated for fifty years.

Mrs. Canton shared with the guys that she's a widow and has lived here for sixty years. This is the second house she has ever lived in. Her husband of sixty-one years passed away last year, and she can't leave this place now.

Tuttle moved the conversation ahead by sharing the news about her neighbor. As soon as the words left his mouth, tears streamed down Mrs. Canton's face.

"I can't believe this. It's the boy that's from prison, isn't it? I told Hazel to be careful. You know she taught him in grammar school. She told me years ago that boy was trouble."

"Mrs. Canton, do you know Augustus?" Taylor inquired as he studied her face.

"Oh, no, I don't. I mean, I know him when I see him, but I've never spoken to him, and I never will. I can't believe he killed Hazel. We've been neighbors and friends for years. Now, what will I do?" Another round of fresh tears started as she patted her face with a tissue.

Once the guys felt they had all the information Mrs. Canton offered, they left her with her memories. Then, after a few additional stops and with no one home, they left more cards tucked into door frames than they had spoken to people.

Mrs. Canton proved to be the most knowledgeable. They confirmed Hazel taught at the county grammar school for years. Taylor wonders if the Sheriff had her for a teacher.

Tuttle broke the silence, "what are the odds Sherriff Steele had Hazel for a teacher?"

"That thought crossed my mind, too. I hope for her sake she didn't. She's been through so much for this guy. Hazel might be the tipping point." Taylor shared as he rubbed his neck. Tension knots grew by the hour, and no amount of rubbing would remove them.

The deputies returned to the office and added Hazel's information to the board. Taylor glanced at his notes and said, "I'll call Maddox and Bud. They need to know the latest."

Tuttle walked off to the bullpen as Taylor pulled his cell phone from his pants pocket. He sat down in the Sheriff's desk chair and took deep breaths. He wanted his mind ready for the conversations. Taylor dialed Maddox first.

Maddox answered on the second ring. "Maddox, Deputy Taylor. We just returned from another crime scene involving our escapee. Hazel Poller, a retired schoolteacher, died at the hand of Augustus or his crew. Sal, the owner of the Snappy Mart, spotted Augustus pumping gas overnight. He called it into the Sheriff, but in her absence, Deputy Tuttle and I responded. Someone slashed Hazel's throat, ear to ear and stole her vehicle. That's how we found her lying on her kitchen floor."

"I can't believe it. Another murder." Maddox sighed. "You said he stole a vehicle. What's the description?"

"He has a 2010 gold Toyota van in his possession. I'll text the description with the tag number. We found Hazel forty-eight hours after her demise." Taylor tapped the texting button, and off it went.

Taylor heard the beep through the phone, knowing his text had made it. Maddox stated, "text received. Now for my updates. Jermaine and Duke have bogus addresses on their driver's licenses. I'm unsure how that happened. We uncovered the fact that Jermaine's dad still lives in the county. We visited with him yesterday and learned nothing. Jermaine's dad kicked him out of the house at eighteen years old when he found boxes of marijuana stored under his bed. He hasn't seen or spoken to him since." Maddox rustled papers while waiting for a reply.

"I have nothing else. We'll reach out later." Before Taylor could end the call, Maddox asked about the Sheriff's condition. Taylor gave him a quick reply since there was no change.

With Maddox's update out of the way, Taylor called Ivey. He wanted to catch both, so he only had to say the updates once. Now, he understood why the Sheriff gets frustrated with the case updates.

Taylor prepared his notes as Ivey's phone rang so he could give the most concise updates to the pair. Ivey didn't answer her phone, which sent chills up Taylor's spine. He dialed Bud, and the same happened. What if something happened to the Sheriff?

Taylor jumped up from the desk and found Tuttle typing reports in the bullpen. "Tuttle. Where are the guys, Johnson and Long?"

"Long is riding with Johnson and Rufus today. His training is about to end. Do you know if the Sheriff will keep him on board? She usually rides with the new deputies a few days before deciding. I guess you can do that since you've ridden with him before."

"Long rode with me for two weeks before we started rotation. I suppose I could ride with Long for a few shifts and ensure he understands his role." Taylor looked down as he considered his options.

Taylor shook his head as he remembered why he approached Tuttle. "That's not why I'm here. I called Bud and Ivey, and neither answered their phones. So, I'm heading to the hospital. With these updates, I can deliver them in person and check on the Sheriff. Do you want to tag along if Scarlett is working?" Taylor winked at Tuttle as he mentioned Scarlett.

Tuttle's eyes glazed over as he thought of Scarlett. "She's working. Let's go." Tuttle rolled his chair backward, stood, and locked his computer in one fluid movement. It impressed Taylor.

The duo waved goodnight to Maggie as she left the office for the day. They jumped into Taylor's patrol car and drove to the hospital. Bud and Ivey were not in the waiting room, and something niggled at Taylor's neck. He looked over at Tuttle, and he felt the same sensation.

"Tuttle, do you feel someone is watching us?"

"Yes, I've had the sensation since we stepped out of the car in the parking lot. The strange part is I see no one. There isn't a nurse walking down the hallway or anything. I'll call Scarlett."

Within seconds, Scarlett approached Taylor and Tuttle from the elevator. "Come on, guys. Follow me." She waved her hand at the duo, and when Tuttle got close enough, she reached up and peeked at him on the cheek.

Taylor winked at Tuttle and followed Scarlett to the elevator. "Sheriff Steele is downstairs having another CT scan. The doctors wanted to confirm everything was okay because she still hadn't woken. They thought she should be awake by now. The longer she stays in the coma, the more concerned they become. Ivey and Bud are waiting outside the exam room."

After Scarlett's explanation, Taylor didn't know what to say, so he kept quiet. How could something like this happen to the Sheriff? When the elevator came to a rest, the doors slid open. Scarlett turned right. Then a left down a hallway. Bud and Ivey leaned against the wall with their arms crossed against their chests and heads resting on the wall.

Chapter 11

Bud was the first to recognize movement. He tapped Ivey on the arm. "Taylor is here." Ivey stood and fell into Taylor's arms.

"I'm so worried about Jada. The doctors decided on another CT scan because she remains in a coma." Words tumbled out of Ivey's mouth as Taylor stroked the back of her head. Taylor looked at Bud, and Bud shrugged his shoulders. He couldn't help Ivey feel better because his insides were slowly dying.

Scarlett tried to make the group feel better by saying the doctors just wanted another look at the Sheriff. They suspect nothing to be wrong. The group nodded, but no one answered. Tuttle took Scarlett's hand, and they stepped away from the group. They whispered for a few minutes before Scarlett left.

Bud eyed Tuttle. "Tuttle, do you and Taylor have news for us? We could use something else to think about."

"Taylor spoke with Maddox already, and we wanted you two to hear the news. He tried calling you, but neither answered your phones." Tuttle explained as he looked at Taylor.

Ivey looked at Taylor, then at Tuttle. "Can we talk here? I want to hear the updates, but I don't want to leave Jada. We've been here almost two hours, so it shouldn't be much longer."

Taylor glanced around and saw no one. "It's so quiet down here. I see no reason we can't discuss it here. We can pick up where we left off later if the doctor comes out."

With his notes in his hands, Taylor described Sal's call, the visit to the store, and the video of Augustus pumping gas. Bud sucked in a breath as Ivey's eyes grew wide. Then, Taylor told of Hazel's murder. It forced all the air from Bud and Ivey's lungs.

Bud paced as he ran his fingers through his hair. Ivey has tears sitting on the brink of overflowing. The most promising piece of evidence is the bloody shoe print. Taylor ended the updates with information on Duke and Jermaine's bogus addresses.

"I need to make sure I heard everything. Augustus and his boy murder a lady, steal her vehicle, leave us a bloody shoe print, get caught on camera pumping gas at the Snappy Mart, and Duke and Jermaine have bogus addresses on their driver's licenses." Bud's face turned red, and the veins in his neck protruded.

Taylor and Tuttle stepped back as they expected Bud's lid to blow. Taylor took the brunt of the exchange. "I can't believe anyone feels this is an update. This proves we are no closer to finding Augustus. Our prison boy has a new ride. Isn't that swell?" Bud placed both hands on the wall and lowered his head. Ivey patted him on his back and whispered to him, but he didn't flinch or turn around.

As the group stared at one another, the opening double doors made a swoosh as a nurse wheeled the Sheriff into the hallway. A doctor followed the gurney. When he saw the group, he stopped and stated, "there are no recent issues. Sheriff Steele makes her own timetable. Her vitals are normal, so it's a waiting game for us. She could wake in one minute or one month."

"One month?" Bud whispered.

"I said that to make a point. Not to say she won't wake before then. Everyone reacts differently to head injuries. Be patient." The doctor reiterated.

The group followed the nurse upstairs to the Sheriff's room and waited while the nurses hooked her up to her machines. Taylor leaned over to the others and said, "can I bring supper for either of you? I'm heading back to the office."

Bud and Ivey shook their heads from side to side. Taylor looked at Ivey. "We'll talk later." He turned with Tuttle on his heels and almost made it to the elevator when Bud called him. Taylor groaned, and Tuttle chuckled as they waited for Bud.

"Taylor, I need to apologize for my outburst. This case is frustrating me, and I know it frustrates us all. I get that. Thanks for coming by with the updates. Call if you need anything." Bud reached out and shook hands with Taylor and Tuttle. Taylor nodded. He was still mad at the way Bud reacted. Does Bud think the case is at a standstill since he and Ivey are away?

When Taylor and Tuttle finally made it outside, Taylor sighed. Then Tuttle spoke. "Bud went overboard with the outburst. Does he realize you can withhold the updates? He better not make you mad." Tuttle pointed out the obvious.

A grin spread across Taylor's face. "I think I'll let him call me for updates. Let's see how long it takes before I get the first call. Or, he will have Ivey call me for the updates." Taylor shook his head. "Bud's attack shouldn't make me mad, but it did. He had no reason to yell."

Scarlett walked out of the hospital and grinned when she saw the guys standing on the curb. Taylor waved and said his goodbyes to Tuttle and Scarlett. He wanted to get back to the office, anyway. But instead of the office, Taylor drove to the Snappy Mart. He wanted to survey the area and look for signs of Augustus. With dusk approaching, Augustus and his boys might be on the move. Taylor passed through the woods where Tonya Zon died. Every time he traveled this road, unpleasant memories returned. The same happened when he gave the warehouses where a killer held Ivey hostage. The city council voted to demolish those warehouses after a six-month negotiation. So, they no longer stand. Taylor can only hope those memories of Ivey's capture subside.

On Taylor's approach to the office, his radio squawked. He paused and waited for the dispatcher to state the call. As he listened to the dispatcher mention a gold Toyota van, his pulse picked up, and he grabbed the mic from its holder. "Dispatch, this is Taylor. Show me en route to the last call." Taylor spun the car onto the roadway and pressed the pedal. Then, while driving with one hand, he picked up the mic and called the Georgia State Patrol officer chasing Augustus.

The officer responded and described the area he spotted the gold Toyota. Then the officer lets loose on a string of obscenities. Taylor continued speeding to the area when the officer admitted he had lost the van. The officer and Taylor pulled alongside each other at the county line, and Taylor asked the officer to describe what happened.

"I was driving westbound as the gold van passed me going eastbound. I activated lights and sirens, made a U-turn, and then I lost the van. The only way the driver lost me was to enter the interstate by turning right to head north on I75." The officer stated.

Taylor's head swung toward the interstate entrance ramp, then back to the GSP officer. "Jump on the interstate and take the next exit. At the end of the exit ramp, go left. Then call me while you continue driving. I'm heading in the other direction. We should meet in thirty minutes on Rt 3." Taylor didn't wait for a reply. He already had the lights and sirens activated and had pulled away from the meeting place.

With the flashing lights on the roof of his car, drivers pulled over as Taylor sped past. He continued to Rt 3 and slid into the turn. The tires grabbed the asphalt and kept the car in his lane. As the road loomed long in the distance, trees passed the car in a blur.

Minutes later, the GSP officer spoke over the radio. Taylor listened to the officer tell the dispatcher he had no sign of the gold Toyota. Picking up the mic, Taylor keyed it for dispatch, advising his location. With frustration in his actions, he slapped the control for his lights and sirens. But as Taylor drove further down the road, he checked each side because his gut told him Augustus was in the area. Did Augustus move his campsite to this side of the river?

An hour later, Taylor stopped in at the office. He had nothing to show for his efforts, but with the GSP officer spotting the vehicle, he had proof Augustus remained in the area. That's more than he had yesterday.

Nighttime at the Sheriff's office is quiet. He understood why Sheriff Steele came into the office during the overnight hours. It makes for the perfect time to get things done. Taylor sat in the Sheriff's chair as he approved reports and made work assignments. Tomorrow, Deputy Long rejoins the day shift to ride with Taylor.

With all administrative duties handled, Taylor left for the night. When he slid into the driver's seat, he realized he hadn't spoken with Ivey tonight. He pulled his phone from his pocket. While his finger was in motion to press Ivey's speed dial button, he closed his phone. She'll be with Bud, and he doesn't want to deal with him tonight. But he wondered about the Sheriff's condition.

Taylor made it home and climbed into bed with so many thoughts that he wasn't sure what to think. Eventually, he fell into a dream-filled sleep. He and Ivey chased Augustus while Jada and Bud watched on the sideline. The sheriff smiled at him when he glanced at her.

With an alarm sounding, Taylor rolled over and squinted as he read the clock on his phone. Then he moaned. How can it be daytime already? His body felt achy and tired, but he pushed himself to move. Without the Sheriff, he couldn't stay home. He had too many people counting on him today.

After a shower, Taylor felt somewhat human. As he dressed, his cellphone rang. He grinned when he saw the caller. "Good morning, beautiful." He answered.

"Ah, Damon Taylor. That's sweet. I didn't hear from you last night. Everything okay?" Ivey asked.

"Yes. Last night, a GSP officer spotted Augustus in the gold van, but he lost him. I drove around looking for him for two hours. I finally gave up and went to the office. Now, I'm on my way to ride with Deputy Long. He's in the last week of field training. How's the Sheriff?"

Ivey described the overnight events, and it gave Taylor hope. "Bud was with Jada at daybreak when she moaned and moved on the bed. Bud calmed her

143

by rubbing her arm and talking with her. The doctor said her moans and movement are signs of recovery."

"That's great, Lana. I'll stop by today and check on her. Talk later." Taylor wore a smile as he entered the Sheriff's office.

Deputy Long stood at Maggie's desk as Taylor passed. "Good Morning. Anything happening?" Taylor didn't stop at Maggie's because he knew she would follow him into the office.

When Taylor turned around to sit, Maggie and Long stood at his desk. He chuckled. Maggie handed him a few messages. The media are aware of Augustus and the murders and want to talk to someone. Taylor grimaced. He wished the press would leave them alone. After Maggie returned to her desk, Deputy Long said, "ready to ride, sir?"

Taylor laid the messages on the desk and stood to leave with Long when his cellphone rang. He glanced down at the caller ID and said, "Maddox."

"Taylor. I'm meeting the Jackson State Prison Warden in about ten minutes. I called to see if you would be available to meet around lunch because I should have an update."

"Sure. I'm riding with Deputy Long today, so I can't say where we'll be, but call me when you make it back to the county. We'll figure it out from there."

Long looked at Taylor and wondered what was on the man's mind. Taylor wore an odd expression. Maybe the stress of the job bothered him. Deputy Long would not let that cloud his day because his excitement was apparent. His grin stretched across the lower half of his face, causing his eyes to turn to slits.

Taylor said, "Where are we going, Deputy Long?"

"Patrol, sir. Patrol. That is until we receive a call."

The duo climbed into the car, and Long made a right turn out of the parking lot. Without uttering a word, Long drove Taylor down Rt 3. It's almost as if Long knew about last night. Taylor glanced over at Long, but Long acted like this was a routine trip.

Over the next few hours, the guys responded to multiple emergency calls. First, they had two accidents, one of which had severe injuries. Another call had them scrambling at a home alarm. They first thought Augustus was breaking in, but it turns out the homeowner's daughter skipped school and forgot about the new alarm.

When lunch rolled around, Long mentioned Maddox. Taylor forgot about their lunch meeting. He called Maddox, and his meeting with the warden continued. Maddox agreed to get with Taylor some other time. So, the guys enjoyed lunch as it gave Long a chance to ask questions and make observations about the day.

Taylor suggested they return to the office. Long can write his reports while Taylor returns the call to the media. Then, they'll stop in at the hospital and check on the Sheriff. As they entered the parking lot, Taylor agreed he was ready for the Sheriff to come out of her coma. This job is more extensive than he ever imagined. He needs a few more years of experience before he wants to tackle being a Sheriff.

Deputy Johnson and Tuttle entered the office with Rufus. Taylor and Rufus always play tug of war, and the dog knows it. Rufus spots Taylor and dashes off for his rope. He brings it to Taylor and sits, waiting patiently. By the time Taylor is free, the drool has dropped from both sides of his mouth and collected in small puddles on the floor.

"Johnson, clean up your dog's mess, please. Come on, boy, let's have some fun." Taylor walked the dog into the Sheriff's Office, and their game began. After ten minutes, Taylor collapsed. "Rufus, you're strong. Take a break." Rufus lay beside Taylor's chair.

"Taylor, I'm taking Rufus home before stopping at the hospital. Do you need me for anything else today?" Deputy Johnson asked while holding Rufus' leash.

"I'm stopping by in a few minutes, too. Maybe Long can come with me. Either way, I'll see you at the hospital." Taylor isn't ready to face Bud yet, because he's afraid of his reaction to another verbal confrontation. But he knows he'll have to since he and Bud are dating sisters.

Taylor found Long hunched over his computer, finishing up a report. Long leaned back in his chair with a sigh. "Deputy Long, tell me how you feel about your job." Taylor didn't elaborate on what he hoped to hear.

Long paused before he answered. "I feel blessed to have this opportunity, and I hope Sheriff Steele keeps me on the road. And you, of course. The department makes me feel like I belong. I want to be here to help this county and my fellow deputies in any way possible."

A smile spread across Taylor's face. "That's what I wanted to hear. So, I wrote my recommendation to Sheriff Steele this afternoon, requesting your permanent assignment."

"Are you serious, Taylor? That's excellent news! I can't thank you enough for your time and attention to me." Long's face lit up with pride.

"I'm going to the hospital. You can ride along if you want or go home and share the news with your family." Taylor offered.

Long's head swung from side to side, "I'm going to the hospital, then I'll see, mom."

As the guys walked to the car, Long carried an extra bounce in his step. With Taylor and Long's discussion, Johnson and Tuttle beat them to the hospital. The deputies slid into Sheriff Steele's room just to speak to her. They want her to know they are there for her.

Delight showed on Bud and Ivey's faces as the group descended on them. After the brief visit with the Sheriff, the group moved to the waiting room to talk. The conversation centered on Sheriff Steele. Bud described the bouts of moaning and thrashing that the Sheriff has experienced throughout the day. He emphasized the doctors think the actions are leading her to come out of the coma.

Everyone expressed a grateful heart to hear the news. Just as Taylor and Ivey walked to the far corner of the room, Taylor's cell phone rang. He glanced at the number and grinned. While he spoke to the caller, Ivey caught bits and pieces of the conversation. Her pulse ticked up as she waited for Taylor to end the call.

The duo rejoined the group as Taylor shared, "I just got off the phone with my investigator contact. He wants to meet me in one hour with information about Aidan's killer. Call my cell if anyone needs me."

Ivey spoke, "I'm going with you, Taylor. I want to nail this killer." All eyes turned to Ivey, and they stared. "What? Bud is here. I'll return as soon as I can."

Bud agreed with Ivey. They spoke about Ivey getting back into cases, even though she wanted Jada out of the coma before taking a new case. Bud feels working on this case will help Ivey feel more comfortable with the job again. There have been times he thought she might resign from her post as an FBI agent. He sure hoped not. Ivey is the best partner he has ever worked beside.

"Long, can you ride back to the office with Tuttle or Johnson?"

"Don't worry about me. Go meet this guy and identify our killer!" Long exclaimed.

Ivey and Taylor walked out of the hospital hand in hand and jumped into Taylor's car, buckling their belts in silence. "Thanks for letting me come along," Ivey said to Taylor, then he started the car.

"I'm glad you did. We've had little time alone to talk. How are you coping with Jada's injury? I've been afraid it will jog too many memories for you." Taylor expressed his concern as his eyes grew dark.

Ivey ran her hands down her thighs, took a deep breath, and answered, "I won't lie and say it doesn't bother me because it does. Bud told me how you stayed with me while I was in the hospital. You never told me that. Thank you. I couldn't have made it through that ordeal without you." Ivey explained as her eyes filled to the brink with tears.

"Don't cry, Lana. I didn't want to be anywhere else. That's why Bud refuses to leave too." Taylor reached over, lifting Ivey's hand, and placing the softest kiss on it.

Ivey patted her face with a tissue before replying. "Let's get going before I crumble altogether." Ivey checked her face in the overhead mirror and grimaced. "What causes my eyes to turn red after

just a few tears?" Taylor doesn't respond. He loves
her face anyway he can get it.

Chapter 12

By the time they arrived at their predetermined meeting place, darkness had descended. They met in a small, out-of-the-way diner halfway between their offices, so the law enforcement officers were out of their jurisdiction.

Taylor spotted his contact, sitting with his back to the wall at a corner table. He lifted his tea glass in acknowledgment of Taylor's arrival. The man raised his eyebrows when they approached the table, realizing Ivey was along for the meeting.

After the introductions, they settled in for the update. Taylor's contact shared information about their potential killer. He described the guy physically and added his name as Micah Stutter. Micah has been in and out of jail since his juvenile days. His rap sheet is extensive. The most potent of crimes was the incident that occurred six years ago. At seventeen years old, as he drove a vehicle belonging to another person, he struck and killed a bicyclist. The police tracked the car, which led to the driver and a charge of vehicular manslaughter. They couldn't prove DUI or drugs since they didn't find him until two weeks after the incident.

Micah is a well-liked car mechanic. He has a brilliant mind for motors and how they operate. Now, he repairs vehicles, paints them, and restores old cars to look new.

As a child, Micah was in and out of the foster care system. None of his foster parents could contain him because he always rebelled against instructions from his parents or teachers. He was a high school dropout in the tenth grade and started his first job as a mechanic.

After Taylor's contact took a break and sipped his tea, Taylor asked, "do you know where he lives or his mechanic shop? We want to talk with him."

The man passed Taylor a piece of paper with Micah's photo and contact information. "This is the last known address of his shop and apartment. Just remember, this guy has been on his own for years. He's a fixer and will fix whatever he needs to survive."

Ivey stated, "So, a little blood on his hands is nothing to him."

"Precisely, Agent Ivey." The contact excused himself and left Ivey and Taylor sitting at the table nursing a glass of sweet tea. They stared at Micah's photo.

"How do you want to handle this, Taylor? Without backup, I'm not sure we need to visit this guy tonight." Ivey made her point.

Taylor nodded, "I agree. Besides, I must let Micah's sheriff know our plans before acting on the information. With Sheriff Steele out, I can't afford to make things rough on her when she returns."

The duo returned to their county with relief, knowing they had Aidan's killer and the person responsible for Louisa's injuries. Ivey made a mental note to check on Louisa. Since the incident with Jada, she hasn't checked on anyone, not even Taylor.

The radio crackled, and they shared a glance. Seconds passed when the dispatcher toned to the fire department. An apartment building downtown burns with flames visible from the main street. "Wow. It's something all the time now. This county used to be quiet with few criminals or emergencies. Now, things happen constantly."

"That means your county is growing. The people must like it here. I know I do." Ivey smiled, and her eyes sparkled.

"Here we are, Ivey. I'll walk you up. I'm not taking any chances." Taylor took Ivey's hand, and he escorted her to Sheriff Steele's room. When they opened the door, they witnessed Bud whispering to Jada to calm down. Ivey rushed to her side.

As soon as Jada heard Ivey, her body released the tension and settled into a deep sleep. "What happened?" Ivey directed the question to Bud.

"I stepped away to the bathroom, and when I returned, she was thrashing about in the bed again. You walked in right after I returned. I'm glad you did. She settled when she heard your voice." Bud stroked Jada's hair as she slept. Taylor backed out of the room as his phone rang.

He answered it to silence the ring. Maddox called and requested they meet in the morning around 10:00 at the sheriff's office. Maddox asked about Jada, and while Taylor replied, he noticed Bud's stare because his eyes drew to slits. Seeing the expression on Bud's face, Taylor exited Jada's room while talking on the phone. He would deal with Bud later.

Without glancing back, Taylor headed home. He needed downtime. Between Sheriff Steele's injury and the two cases, his body told him to slow down. Taylor wanted a chance to sit and think about each case. He doesn't understand why the US Marshalls haven't found Augustus yet. Then, after he arranges for the apprehension of Micah Stutter, one case will be off of his plate.

When Taylor arrived home, things seemed strange. He couldn't describe the feeling. At first, he thought someone had been inside his house, but his alarm remained activated. He stepped out the back door and surveyed the surroundings. Nothing moved or sounded, and he noticed nothing disturbed. So Taylor wrote it off as paranoia and went back inside. He changed into shorts and a t-shirt and strolled down the hall to the kitchen.

Just as he stepped into the kitchen, movement at the kitchen window caught his attention. He instinctively went for his weapon, which he wasn't wearing since he had changed his clothes. Taylor turned and sprinted to his bedroom for his gun. Instead, he hooked his gun belt around his waist and returned to the kitchen.

With the house dark, he peeked out each window, looking for a prowler. When he spotted no one, he exited the house by the garage door. He searched his garage, then moved to the front yard, followed by the back. Once he completed the search, it satisfied him, and he returned inside, but his mind wouldn't stop churning. Finally, he gave up and went to bed, hoping to sleep.

In deep sleep, Taylor wakes to the sound of his phone. He snatches it from the bedside table and mumbles, "Taylor." When he heard the call from dispatch, his eyes flew open.

"I'm on my way," Taylor exclaimed. While dressing, he placed his phone on speaker and dialed Tuttle, Long, and Johnson. This call required backup. The deputies agreed on a staging location and set fifteen minutes for their meeting time.

Taylor couldn't believe the street racers were at it again, not after the debacle with Louisa and Aidan. He wondered if Micah Stutter was the instigator. Taylor pulled Micah's photo from his book and snapped a photo with his phone. Then he texted the picture to the guys. If Micah was at the street race, he wanted him. Hopefully, they can arrest Micah in their county, saving them from coordinating with another county for his arrest.

Once the deputies met at their staging location, Taylor described the incident and texts. He confirmed he didn't know if this race involved Micah, but if he did, he wanted to arrest Micah for Aidan's murder and Louisa's injury.

"Deputy Long, this is your first solo run. Do you feel comfortable? If not, let me know. If you decide to stay back, it will not change your status in the department. Just know we're heading in fast."

Deputy Long looked around at his partners. "If you'll have me, I'm in." He grinned as he waited.

Taylor lifted his hand for a fist bump. "Gear up, wear your ballistic vest, and have your shotgun handy. We'll separate into teams, and Deputy Long, you're with me. Two cars will come from this direction while the others will travel from the other end of Ringer Road. I want to box him. After that, we should have no problem corralling the street racers with four vehicles."

They listened as tires screeched in the distance, and people cheered. Energy increased in anticipation of their upcoming activity. The guys concentrated on their plan as they studied Micah's photo. Each deputy wanted the chance to capture this killer.

Taylor and Long prepared to drive toward the street racers, with Tuttle and Johnson approaching from the opposite direction. Then, Taylor gave the go-ahead over the radio, and all four patrol cars activated lights and sirens simultaneously. The sirens and the flashing lights will shock the racers and the spectators.

As the deputies drove closer to the action, people ran for their cars as they tried to escape the police. People screamed for their friends, and they yelled at the deputies with their fists in the air. The two street racers failed to stop their engines on command.

They fled from the deputies and headed straight into Tuttle's and Johnson's path.

Taylor alerted his deputies to the event and readied themselves for the contact. Moments later, the radio comes to life. "Taylor, Tuttle. The driver of the black car turned around and was heading your way. The other car traveled across a pasture and then re-entered the roadway." Silence. Then Tuttle exclaimed, "he's headed straight for us." Silence.

When no one spoke, Taylor picked up his mic. "Tuttle, Johnson, status."

Taylor avoided a collision with the driver of the black car. Long glanced through his window and watched the black swerve. Long approached the left rear quarter panel and attempted a pit maneuver. The driver saw him approach and tried to evade contact, but the car spun out of control when Taylor struck the vehicle from the other side. It struck a tree with the left front, rendering the car and driver disabled.

"Long, check on the driver. If he needs an ambulance, call one but stay with him. Wear your shoulder radio. Good job." Taylor stated, then he said, "Tuttle, Johnson, status."

Crackling sounds came over the radio. "Johnson here. Micah was the driver of the dark blue car. I identified him when he turned the car around in the roadway. We're following him back toward you. He's flying, Taylor. If he hits another car, he'll kill someone else. This guy is crazy."

"Stop him. Can you shoot his tire?" Taylor asked.

Both deputies replied, "10-4." Thirty seconds later, Taylor watched the flashing lights grow closer by the second. Finally, a gunshot echoed in the night. Then, "Tuttle here. Johnson shot the tire, but the car hit a pothole. We're unsure if the bullet hit."

"Pit maneuver, NOW," Taylor shouted.

Johnson was the first car to gain on the driver. He struck the left rear with the right front of his car. The driver tried to avoid the contact but misjudged the distance. When Johnson hit his car, he began spinning, no longer controlling the vehicle. The vehicle came to rest in the ditch with the driver's side door flat against the dirt.

Luckily for the deputies, both accidents were close enough together that the deputies could monitor both. Tuttle reached the car first, yelled at the driver to throw out his weapon, and placed his hands on the steering wheel. He complied.

Deputy Long sprinted to the second accident scene, reached inside the car, and plucked Micah Stutter from the driver's seat by his shirt collar. Micah could not defend himself against Deputy Long's strength as his feet dangled above the ground before Long dropped him into the dirt.

Taylor looked at his guys. "that was spectacular work, guys. Someone read Micah his rights. He'll spend a few nights with us." Taylor walked off to visit with the ambulance EMTs.

The EMTs shared with Taylor that the racer was unconscious and had a broken leg. They'll transport him to the hospital for treatment. Taylor advised he'd follow and remain with the driver until a deputy arrived to stay with him. This guy will spend a few nights in jail once he recovers.

Once the ambulance pulled away, Taylor walked back to his group. "I'm going to the hospital with racer number 1. Take Micah to our jail and book him. I'll fill out the paperwork tomorrow. Go home and get some sleep. You're still on duty tomorrow."

Tuttle spoke up. "I'm going with you to the hospital. Scarlett is on nights this week. Since I'm awake, I might as well stop in and say hello." Tuttle grinned as he turned red.

The guys chuckled at Tuttle's expense. Taylor wonders if he turns red when he talks about Ivey. Since he's going to the hospital, he'll slip upstairs and check on Ivey and the Sheriff. He liked Tuttle's way of thinking.

Taylor and Tuttle pulled away and headed to the hospital in tandem. Both men were tired from the exertion and the adrenaline rush, but they wanted to visit their ladies. Once they reached the hospital, they entered through the emergency department. Taylor stepped over to the counter since his first obligation was the street racer's condition. His driver was in surgery to repair a broken leg. Taylor advised the nurse another deputy would arrive to stay with the driver until they could move him to jail.

159

After speaking with the nurse, Taylor stepped into the waiting room corner and texted Ivey. He doesn't want to insert himself into a strained situation in the middle of the night. Seconds later, he received a message telling him to come upstairs. Ivey has a surprise. He rereads the message to make sure he saw it correctly.

With trembling hands, Taylor pressed the button for the elevator. The hospital was quiet, and he rode the elevator alone. Ivey waited for him when the doors opened. Ivey whispered, "hurry." She reached out, taking Taylor's hand as she pulled him into Sheriff Steele's room.

"Taylor, what are you doing here at this hour?" Sheriff Steele asks.

Tears build in Taylor's eyes as they grow wide, then he breaks into a huge grin. "This is the best surprise!" Taylor walked over to Jada and hugged her while sitting on the bed. "When did all of this happen?"

"In the night, I decided it was time to come back. I woke up like nothing happened until Bud told me how long I had been here."

"How do you feel? You look great. Your cheeks have color again, and your eyes are bright. I think you will be out of here in no time." Taylor said.

Then Ivey said, "her doctor knows she's awake, and they want to run more tests before letting her out, but things look great." Ivey squeezed Taylor's hand.

Bud looked around the group, "why are you here in the middle of the night?" Bud asked with a bit of concern in his voice.

Taylor explained the circumstances that brought him to the hospital. Sheriff Steele perked up when she heard about Micah's arrest. But then her eyebrows drew together like something popped into her brain.

Ivey noticed it too, "Jada. What's wrong? Do I need to get the doctor for you?"

"No. I just remembered Louisa is in this hospital too. Has anyone checked on her progress? What's the status on Augustus?" Sheriff Steele asked.

Taylor answered, "Louisa is recovering while still in a coma since her body accepts treatment. Augustus remains at large, and I have a meeting today with Maddox. He visited with the warden, and he had information to share. With luck, the warden gave Maddox places to search for Augustus."

Sheriff Steele nodded in agreement. "Taylor, I can't thank you enough for stepping up when I went down. I would never have guessed Augustus would slug me on my walk into the medical examiner's office. I'll thank Tuttle and Long for finding me when they did." Sheriff Steele reached up and dabbed her eyes with a tissue.

"Sheriff, I've told you before, you need not worry about the office. We've got this. I need to get going because I can't wait to tell the office the news! I'll catch up with you later in the day."

Bud thanked Taylor as he walked from the room. Ivey trailed behind him. She walked him all the way to the emergency room exit. "Ivey, I don't want you going outside alone. I'll stop over later. Thanks for letting me see Sheriff Steele. We're ready for her return to duty."

With a kiss, Taylor exited the hospital and climbed into his car. Instead of going to the office, he opted for home and a few hours of sleep before his official workday began. While walking to the car, an ambulance roared into the emergency entrance, followed by a personal car. Taylor watched in wonder as the EMTs unloaded the patient and wheeled them inside. He lifted a silent prayer for all the parties involved. Taylor figured he owed them a prayer since he received an answer to one of his.

Taylor fell asleep as his head hit his pillow. For three hours, he slept so soundly he never heard his alarm. The sounding of a ringing phone jarred him awake. He searched for his phone and found it on the floor beside his bed. Glancing at it, he grimaced as he answered.

"Taylor." Then he waited.

"Maddox, yes, I'll be there. I had a late night. Before you hear it from someone else, Sheriff Steele came out of her coma overnight. She looks and sounds terrific." Taylor explained his late arrival at the office.

There was silence on the other end of the phone as Maddox composed himself. Taylor heard the emotion in Maddox's voice as he said, "That's great news, Taylor. Thank you for sharing. I'm not sure anyone else would have. I'll see you at ten." Maddox ended the call without waiting for a reply.

Maddox's reaction caught Taylor off guard. He knew Maddox had powerful feelings for Sheriff Steele, but he didn't realize the depth of those feelings. Does Sheriff Steele feel the same way? Would she let Bud go for Maddox? Taylor couldn't let the thoughts go surrounding Maddox and Sheriff Steele and how Ivey would handle the news.

Chapter 13

Taylor called Maggie and gave her the update on Sheriff Steele. She broke down into happy tears, which were expected given their relationship. He asked her to call the office together for the announcement.

When Taylor entered the bullpen, people stood shoulder to shoulder. He included the jail division and the dispatchers in this meeting. "Good morning. I need to update you on Sheriff Steele, and this was the fastest way possible. Overnight, she awoke from her coma. I've seen her and spoken to her. She'll have more tests today to ensure everything is going in the right direction, and then they'll release her home. Another prayer was answered. Now, get to work." Taylor watched his group's shoulders drop as they clapped with the news.

Maggie brought Taylor coffee just as she does for the Sheriff. "Here are a few phone messages for you. Some referenced the street race last night." Taylor looked at Maggie.

"No wonder the Sheriff caters to you. No one in this chair could keep it all straight without you." Maggie beamed with the recognition. Then Taylor continued with last night's episode into the street racer debacle.

"So, Aidan and Louisa's family will have closure. Great work, Taylor. It will delight the Sheriff too.

I'm going to the hospital if that's okay. I just need to see the Sheriff." Maggie pleaded. "I'll be right back."

"Go on. Give her another hug for me. I'm meeting Maddox here at ten, so we'll be in the conference room for a while. Now, all our concentration will turn to Augustus and his guys."

After Maggie left, Taylor reviewed last night's reports from Long, Tuttle, and Johnson. Now, he must take the time to write his version. He had the hospitalized driver's information to add to his report. Taylor posted a deputy at the guy's door, but he wouldn't be going anywhere, anytime soon, with his injuries.

Louisa and Aidan popped into Taylor's mind as he thought about last night. He picked up the phone and dialed the number for Aidan's dad. He answered on the second ring. Taylor spent thirty minutes rehashing the previous night's events. Mr. Turner expressed his gratitude for a job well done. Then he did the same for Louisa's family. Taylor spoke with her mother, and he went through the same explanation as he did with Mr. Turner. Both families expressed relief knowing Micah was off the streets, and he will be for many years.

Taylor treated himself to another cup of coffee, and when he passed the lobby, he watched Maddox enter the front door. Taylor waved him into his office so that he could gather his notes on Augustus. Then they would move to the conference room, which had much more space.

"Maddox, follow me. I need to stop by my office before we go to the conference room." Taylor said as he walked down the hall.

The duo entered the office, then turned around and headed for the conference room. "What's in your box, Maddox? That looks like an awful lot of paperwork." Taylor said with a chuckle.

"It is a lot. The warden gave me additional information yesterday on Augustus, plus, I have background checks on the guards." Maddox placed the box on the table and opened the lid.

Taylor glimpsed inside and saw that Maddox wasn't kidding. The box contained stacks of paper. They removed the piles, then sorted them according to the topic. Augustus was topic number one. Then the guards followed. Taylor sipped coffee as he picked up half of the Augustus stack and began reading. Maddox followed Taylor's lead.

Over the next two hours, the duo read everything on Augustus, and they took pages of notes. Some information shocked them because no one mentioned it in an earlier communication.

When he read the last one, Taylor laid his pen down on the table, reviewed his notes, and glanced at Maddox. "How come no one mentioned Augustus and Lyle Fins attended the same high school? That is a pivotal piece of information and one we needed to follow."

"I agree. That would have been nice to know early in the search. It's hard to believe Augustus was a model prisoner after acclimating to life inside. The notes state he became a leader of his block by offering protection to those less fortunate in stature."

Taylor continued, eyeing his notes. "I've got a note saying the guards searched his cell after the escape and found money stashed under his cot in the far corner, tied by kitchen string. Wonder why he left it, and how did he get cash?" Then Taylor turned the page in his book. "It also stated they found sketches of landscapes with rivers and sketch pencils under his mattress. I think Sheriff Steele and Bud witnessed Duke accept a drawing from Augustus on one of his many visits."

Maddox drew his eyebrows together. "Does that signify anything? What would Duke want with a landscape sketch?" The thought niggled at the back of Maddox's brain, but he let it go because they had more reading to finish.

Next, the duo moved on to the guards. Each guard had a separate report with nothing useful until they spotted Lyle Fin's report. Taylor couldn't wait until he finished it. "This report says Lyle lives near the prison in a wealthy part of town. He also drives a $70,000 SUV. Now, where does a prison guard get that kind of cash?"

Looking at the report Taylor passed to him, Maddox stated, "that makes little sense. He couldn't afford that unless he received a significant inheritance, and from what I hear of his family, they don't have that kind of money either."

Taylor stood and paced the room. He glanced at the board holding Augustus' picture with Duke and Jermaine tacked to each side. Ideas ran through his head with landscape pictures, Lyle's relationship with Augustus, and Lyle's lifestyle. These things mean something, but Taylor couldn't put it together yet.

Then Maddox added to their recent information, "Augustus had the same visitors for the two years in prison, but he never asked for a phone call. Why?" Then Maddox looked over at Taylor. "can I view the prison videos that Sheriff Steele watched? I want to see the picture exchange."

"I don't see why not." Taylor leaned over the center of the table and pushed the call button for Maggie. She appeared in the doorway instead of answering the call. "Hi, Maggie. Can you get Augustus' prison videos from Sheriff Steele's email and forward them to me? Maddox and I want to watch them."

"Sure thing. Give me a minute to log in and send them over. I think Bud snipped portions of the video and sent them to the lab, but I'm unsure about his request." Maggie disappeared.

While the guys waited for the videos, they discussed their options. After a back and forth, Maddox plucked his phone from his pocket and dialed a number. He waited for the call to go through. Once answered, he requested financials on Lyle Fins. They wanted to know if Lyle helped Augustus escape prison. If so, they would arrest him too and send him to the same prison he once helped guard.

Taylor had a thought. "Lyle is due back today from his fishing trip. How about we take a ride to Jackson tomorrow and visit Lyle? Now, do we call him and ask for a meeting or show up unannounced?"

"Unannounced. I'd like to catch him unaware and see his facial expression when we share our news."

"I'll go along with that, and I'm riding along. I'll have Deputy Johnson fill in tomorrow for me since I doubt the Sheriff will return that soon." Taylor jotted a reminder on his pad. He glanced at Maddox and noticed worry lines etched on his forehead and around his eyes, but Taylor didn't mention it.

Minutes passed before Maddox shared his dilemma. "Taylor, we've given up on the river campsite. Augustus hasn't returned since my agents ambushed them. My two injured agents are riding desk duty until their doctor removes their stitches. The other ones have done nothing but get mosquito bit."

"I have another area to search. This area is deeper into the woods than the other one, but Augustus left his stolen vehicle in that area, and our BOLO remains outstanding. We'll hike in, so someone with specialized training wouldn't be a bad idea, especially since the first booby-trapped instance." Taylor didn't have to remind Maddox of the circumstance, but Maddox took it in stride.

Maddox nodded about the failed capture and asked, "do you have a map or coordinates for the new area? I'll pass it along to our survivalist. They should have better luck in the woods than the other guys."

"Sure. I can get the coordinates for you and send them to your phone." Taylor took a couple of minutes, then Maddox's phone dings with a text message. After that, Taylor looks at the clock as his stomach growls. The men break for lunch at the diner. They talk a little as they concentrate on food. After the twenty-minute lunch break, the guys climb into Taylor's car and return to the Sheriff's Office.

They enter the conference room, and Taylor notices sticky notes on the table where he last sat. In Maggie's handwriting, she told Taylor the videos were in his email.

"Maddox, the videos are in my email. Do you have time to watch them now? If so, I'm grabbing a coffee. Can I get you one?"

"I'll come along. The videos might help us capture Augustus."

Taylor and Maddox walked to the coffee bar, but a TV news reporter stopped Taylor on the way back. The arrogance of the guy made Taylor furious. If you need something from someone, you shouldn't come at them full force and expect help.

The reporter left empty-handed, and the men returned to their conference room. "That guy had some nerve coming at you as he did. You handled it great, Taylor."

Taylor shrugged his shoulders as he fumed over the confrontation. "Thank you, but I don't understand people like that."

"I could use someone with your skills on my team. If you ever want a change, let me know. The door is always open." Maddox offered. When he looked into Taylor's enormous eyes, it was apparent he had never expected a job offer.

"For right now, I'm good, Maddox. But things change all the time, so I'll stay in touch. Now, let's get to the videos." Taylor clicked the play button, and the guys leaned back in the chairs to watch the show.

They noted the video date, timestamp, and witnessed actions. During the video, they noticed Augustus passing Duke and Jermaine pictures multiple times. All appear to be landscapes with a river. In some pictures, the river winds along a creek bed, but all the pictures have water running over rocks. Some rocks lie on the sides of the river where the bank is taller, and some have water running over rocks under the water.

After the videos, Taylor ponders the significance of the river and the rocks. Why would Augustus draw those pictures with so much detail?

"Maddox, somewhere there is a reason Augustus drew those landscapes. He didn't draw those simply because he enjoyed it. Everything he does has a motive. So why give them to a visitor who stops by several times a week? If he gives away a picture to every visitor, he's passed hundreds over two years."

"That's true. I'm trying to devise a way to inspect several of these landscapes. I wanted to see them up close. That might be his signature in the picture's corner, too. I can't imagine anyone wanting that many signed landscape pictures from Augustus." Maddox stated.

Taylor thought about a way to help Maddox. "We have the FBI in-house now. They have more contacts than we do on technical issues. I'll run it past Ivey. She might have a contact that can help us with that. If the Marshalls Service has a tech group, send it to them, too. We'll take all the help we can get on this."

Maddox agreed with Taylor, and with his eyes down, he asked about Sheriff Steele and her recovery. Taylor shared the doctor's plan to release her today. With Maddox's expression, Taylor approached the tabu subject. "What's your relationship with Sheriff Steele? I know it's none of my business, but in a way, it is because I'm involved with the Sheriff's sister."

"I didn't know that. So, you're dating FBI Agent Ivey. I've had powerful feelings for Sheriff Steele from the moment my eyes saw her. She's an incredible woman. It's a shame Bud got to her first." Maddox started packing the papers again and returning them to his box.

"You have no intention of trying to break them up, right?" Taylor asked without losing eye contact.

"No, I don't because I'm not the type of person who takes another man's girl. I admit I can be arrogant, but it's a show because I'm not that way. I just want to see her happy." Maddox explained, but Taylor saw the emotion flash in his eyes. He loves Sheriff Steele or wants the chance to.

Taylor answered his call without checking caller ID because his mind remained on Maddox and the emotion in his eyes. He heard Maddox, but does he believe what came out of his mouth? Time will tell.

Ivey's voice stirred Taylor to action. "Sorry, Ivey. Maddox and I are finishing up our meeting. Is everything okay?"

Maddox waited for the answer. It concerned him that the situation might involve Jada. He doesn't know if he's strong enough to hold it together if something happens to her. When he watched a grin spread across Taylor's face, Maddox relaxed.

The call ended, and Taylor shared the news with Maddox. "The doctor released her, and Sheriff Steele is on her way home. Sheriff wants to get back to work, but her doctor insists she go home for twenty-four hours. If no headache, she can return to the office on light duty. She can't participate in any form of firearms training until she gets a clean bill of health. Her stitches come out in three days." Taylor's face beamed with the news. He's ready for Sheriff Steele to take over the office again. After his brief stint as interim Sheriff, he isn't sure being a

Sheriff is what he wants in life. Maybe the US Marshalls office is next.

Nodding his agreement, Maddox thanked Taylor for sharing. He shook his hand as his phone rang. Maddox answered, then gave out new orders. The agents on campsite duty moved to a new location while the injured agents took the desks for jobs. They must pull financials on Lyle Fins as Maddox wants those in hand before their trip to Jackson tomorrow.

Maddox waved with the phone nestled between his shoulder and ear and a box tucked under the other arm. He walked out of the conference room as Ivey entered. Ivey waved at him since she didn't want to interrupt his call.

Ivey joined Taylor at the table. He stood and wrapped his arms around her. "You are a sight for sore eyes. I'm glad the Sheriff is on her way home."

"Me too. What a long few days. I can't imagine what you went through with me in the hospital. With Jada's injury, the feelings I'm struggling to suppress have bubbled up. Now, I'm hoping things will settle down. Can you break for lunch, or are you eating with Maddox?"

"We had a bite earlier, but I can go with you if you're hungry. I'm traveling with Maddox tomorrow to Jackson to visit a guard, Lyle Fins. I'll share everything later. Right now, I want us to have some alone time." Taylor winked and took Ivey by the hand. He led her out the side door and held the door to enter the car. Before he pulled out of the lot, he leaned over, and they shared a kiss and a hug, something they hadn't done in a few days.

Taylor and Ivey dropped in on one of their favorite places to dine. The Mexican restaurant has the best food, and it offers outside dining. They walk out onto the patio and take their favorite table. Taylor gets to view the roadway and the customers from his vantage. The napkins have a hard time staying on the table with the breeze. Ivey lets out a soft giggle as Taylor works to control his napkin. After several attempts, he places his tea glass on the napkin stack.

Lunch was short but pleasant. They haven't spent ten minutes alone together since Sheriff Steele's accident. Ivey wanted to hear everything from Augustus. Taylor approached the subject about the landscape photos and how he wanted a close-up view of Augustus' pictures.

Without hesitation, Ivey volunteered for their tech group. She requested the videos by email and will handle the request this afternoon. While preparing to leave the restaurant, dispatch requested patrol deputies to a bar parking lot regarding a car fire. Tuttle and Johnson responded to dispatch. When Taylor heard the reply, he let it go, knowing his deputies would handle the call.

On the return trip to the Sheriff's Office, Tuttle called for Taylor on his cell phone. Taylor braced for the news. They use their cells whenever a deputy has information he doesn't want on the air. "Tuttle, what's up?"

"Taylor, I think you need to see this. We have a burned Toyota van in the parking lot with a burned body in the passenger seat. With the vehicle damaged so severely, Johnson is having difficulty determining the vehicle's color."

"I'll head your way. If Doc James beats me to the scene, don't let him move the body until I see it. I'm dropping Ivey off at the office. Hold on, Tuttle." Taylor turns his head toward Ivey since she tapped his arm.

"Are you sure, Ivey? It's no problem to drop you at the office." Taylor said, then he told Tuttle he and Ivey were on the way.

Chapter 14

Lights flashed, and sirens blared as the duo traveled towards the smoke rising into the sky. The bar sat along Rt 3 at the county's edge. This is a local hangout that has been in business for decades. The parking lot is and always has been gravel and dirt. It's big enough to accommodate eighteen-wheelers and delivery trucks with ample room to circle the building for parking, making for easy access.

At this time of day, the lot will be half full of workers eating lunch and cooling off before returning to their duties. Taylor wondered how the fire started without someone witnessing it.

They entered the lot and pulled in beside Johnson's vehicle. As soon as the doors opened, the smell of burned flesh overtook them. Ivey tried not to gag, but the gag reflex was uncontrollable. "Taylor, go on. I'll be fine." Ivey waved him off as she struggled to compose herself and catch her breath.

Taylor walked over to the guys and pointed to the deceased victim lying in the passenger seat. Johnson verified the burned vehicle was Hazel's, so now Augustus has another new ride. "We need to identify this person, and I bet Augustus is driving their car."

While they waited for the medical examiner's team to show, Taylor and the deputies searched the area, and they spoke to the bar patrons. No one saw

Augustus in the bar, nor did his friends. That idea drew a blank.

The parking lot is full of debris with old cigarette butts, chewing tobacco, and plain trash. There was no way to confirm if the victim disposed of anything, a patron or even Augustus. This crime scene was a nightmare for any crime scene tech.

Doc James and his team walked over to the van, looking at me. "Where's my body?"

Taylor pointed to the car. He watched Doc James shuffle his feet on the way to the van's passenger side. "Bring a bag." He yelled to his staff. "This one is stiff. We'll need help, deputies."

All three deputies shared a glance and shrugged their shoulders. Doc James passed each guy a set of gloves. Once they snapped them in place, they followed Doc James' instructions about lifting and loading a burned body onto a gurney. With every movement, the stench increased. It was the most unpleasant smell any of the men had experienced.

Once they placed the victim on the gurney, the deputies disposed of their gloves. One of the crime scene staff walked over to the guys. "here, rub some of this under your nose. It helps with the stench."

Taylor dipped his fingers inside a tiny green jar of menthol and smeared his upper lip with it. Tuttle and Johnson followed his actions. Each guy took a deep breath and sighed. The pungent smell of menthol is better than the odor of charred flesh.

Doc James approached Taylor and looked over at Ivey as her phone conversation continued. "Taylor, I'll start the work up as soon as I return to the office. I may use dental records to aid in identification. Unfortunately, the victim's fingerprints were of no use. We'll complete the autopsy today or tonight, depending on staffing. I'll call you with the results."

"Thanks, Doc. Call anytime, day or night. The death notification is a top priority."

Once the scene cleared and the tow truck removed the burned vehicle, the deputies returned to their patrol duties. Ivey concluded her call and joined Taylor in the car. "I spoke with the tech department about the landscape pictures. They asked for more clarification about an area of the picture. I asked them to scan the full picture first, then take quadrants and zoom in on those. The extra effort might afford us something."

"Sounds logical to me. Let's get back to the office. I've got reports to write before I can leave for the day." Taylor started the car, looked both ways, and eased onto the roadway.

Ivey's text tone sounded, and she pulled her phone from her pocket. She grinned, then turned to Taylor. "Jada and Bud invited us over this evening. Are you up for a visit?"

Taylor paused before he answered. He still had the issue with Bud hanging over his head. "I'll probably be a little later with the time of day. So why don't you go ahead, and I'll join you as soon as I finish my reports?"

Ivey lifted an eyebrow before asking, "Are you sure you're coming over, or are you giving me an excuse for not showing?" As she waited for an answer, Ivey glared at Taylor from across the seat. She knows the situation with Bud bothered Taylor, but she wanted them to resolve their differences, and she hopes tonight was the start.

"I'll be there. We have a lot happening now, and I'd like to stay on task with my reports. You know how I am about being behind." Taylor smiled and held Ivey's hand for the rest of the drive.

They followed Deputy Long into the parking lot. Long is on the night shift for three more nights, then moves to the day shift. Taylor parked alongside Long, and when they exited their vehicles. Taylor greeted the deputy, "Hey, Long. Can you come to see me before you head out on patrol?"

"Sure thing." Long waved at Ivey as he entered the building.

Taylor and Ivey said their goodbyes. Ivey climbed into her car as Taylor held the door. Once she was on her way to the Sheriff's house, Taylor strolled inside. Long stood at the office door, waiting for Taylor.

Before Long sat in the chair, Taylor described the car fire scene. Long grimaced as Taylor continued ending with the victim's condition. Long's assignment is to patrol the sector around the bar. If anything seems suspicious, investigate it, but call for backup before approaching anyone. If it's Augustus or his guys, killing someone doesn't scare them. He's proven what he can do to another human being.

Taylor does as he promised Ivey. Once he finished his reports, he stopped by his house for a quick shower and a change of clothes. On the ride to the Sheriff's house, he wasn't eager to be in the same room with Bud, but he didn't want to upset Ivey. So, he counted to ten before opening his car door. He hoped ten seconds would be long enough to calm his nerves.

After knocking on the door, he felt a strange sensation standing on the porch. Was someone watching him? His neck hair bristled, giving him a warning sign. However, the front door opened before he spotted the watcher, and I stood on the other side of the threshold, grinning from ear to ear.

When he crossed the threshold to the front door, all warning signs left him. Everyone talked at the same time as when he entered the family room. Ivey stood and kissed his cheek and hugged him. Bud stood off to Ivey's left, and when their exchange ended, he stepped forward with his outstretched hand. Taylor took it, and they shook hands without uttering a word. The sisters exchanged a glance.

The group wandered outside to the patio, just like old times. "After we eat, I want to get an update on everything I missed at work. So, Taylor, get ready. You have a lot of talking to do."

"Yes, Ma'am. I'm ready. You might want to have a notebook handy. We've been an active bunch." Taylor chuckled as he looked at me, and I wondered if he was glad to have me back.

The steaks sizzling on the grill smelled divine. After the burned body, Taylor didn't know if he could swallow food today, but with that smell, who could resist? The couples chatted about my recovery and how miraculous it was to have me back on my feet so soon.

"The strangest part is, I have no memory of getting hit. I can feel the other person's presence behind me, but not the impact. Which, of course, I'm grateful for that." I reached up to my head and ran my fingers over the bandage covering her stitches. "As I woke up, it felt like I had been asleep overnight, not for days." I shared.

"I, for one, am glad you are back to us. You scared us at the beginning. The doctors couldn't explain why you weren't waking up, but I guess your body needed the downtime." Bud's eyes showed the concern he felt.

Once they cleared the dishes from the table, the foursome took to their outdoor chairs. Taylor glanced up and pointed at the moon. "Look how clear the moon is tonight." Everyone took a second and admired God's handiwork. "Are you ready for your updates, Sheriff?"

I chuckled. "I suppose I need to hear it. It might as well be now."

Taylor begins with Micah's arrest. He described the car race, which led to a car chase and finally the arrest of both drivers. Taylor explained that one driver remains in the hospital because of his injuries, but he's expected to recover fully. Then he confirmed Louisa and Aidan's parents were aware of the arrest. Micah lawyered up once we got him to the jail, and he remains there.

Next, Taylor rehashed the latest Augustus sightings. He began with Sal's video of Augustus pumping gas. They discovered the van owner after seeing a partial plate on the van in the video. While conducting a welfare check at her home, they found her body. The deputies spotted a bloody shoe print on the kitchen floor. They hope to match it to Augusts or his crew.

I interrupted. "Sorry to break your rhythm, Taylor. Who owned the van? Are they local?" I looked down at her paper, poised to enter a name.

"Hazel Poller. She was a retired schoolteacher." Taylor waited for a reply, but none came. "Sheriff?"

"I'm sorry, Taylor." I wiped my eyes. "Hazel Poller taught me in elementary school. Do you think Augustus knew that or was she a random target?" My eyes pleaded for an answer as a lone tear rolled down my right cheek.

"I can't answer that, Sheriff. Not until we apprehend Augustus." The group took a break as they sipped their beverages. Ivey nodded at Taylor to continue.

Taylor described the situation with the GSP officer when he spotted Augustus. Finally confessing, Augustus escaped again. Then Taylor detailed his meeting with Maddox and how Maddox spent a half-day with the prison warden. Upon his return, Maddox and Taylor spent hours ciphering the documents from the warden. They watched prison videos zeroing in on the landscape pictures.

Ivey jumped into the conversation and described her request through the FBI tech lab. She hopes to get the enhanced pictures tomorrow.

I questioned the landscape pictures. Ivey explained they couldn't fathom why Augustus passed so many pictures to the same visitors. It made little sense, so they wanted a closer look at the pictures. I nodded in agreement as I jotted notes in her book. This time, I circled the word *landscapes*.

In the end, Taylor told me his plans of traveling with Maddox tomorrow to Jackson to pop in on Lyle Fins. Then he explained his reasons. He covered Lyle's living style with the new SUV purchase compared to his current salary. His reasons for a face-to-face visit with Lyle were understandable.

After I reviewed my notes, I restated some to ensure I had the information correctly. "Sounds like you have it covered, Taylor. I don't know how to thank you for stepping up as you did. I appreciate it, and I won't ever forget it."

"Sheriff, I'm glad you're back. Since I'm leaving early to meet Maddox, I'm heading home. Ivey, stay as long as you like. Just text me when you leave, so I'm prepared for your arrival." Taylor stated as he recalled sleeping with a gun next to his bed since Augustus remained on the run.

"I'll follow you. Jada needs her rest." The couple stood and headed for the door when I placed my hand on Taylor's arm. He stopped and turned to me.

"Be careful tomorrow, Taylor. Call me when you can and tell Maddox hello." Taylor stared at me like my face held the most awkward expression he had ever seen on me. I know he couldn't decide if I was sad about Maddox or confused about my feelings for him.

Taylor and Ivey drove home in silence, mainly because Taylor couldn't get Sheriff Steele's expression out of his head. He wondered how strong Sheriff Steele's feelings were for Maddox. Have Sheriff Steele and Maddox spent time together? Taylor conjures up memories over the past week since Maddox arrived in town, but he can't remember seeing them together. So, if she did, it was in private.

How can they share such a connection without having time to get to know one another? Taylor shook his head as if trying to clear it from the unwanted thought. He reminded himself it's not his place to consider Sheriff Steele's love interest.

As they entered the house, Ivey glanced at Taylor. "What did Jada tell you as we left? Her expression puzzled me."

With a pause and cough, "She told me to be careful tomorrow and call her with an update. I think I shocked her when I mentioned I was traveling with Maddox tomorrow."

Ivey didn't reply, and Taylor didn't ask her thoughts because he thought she had the same ones he had earlier.

When Taylor and Ivey made it home, I laid down in bed. My body hadn't recovered as much as I wanted. It's nice to be home and not in a hospital bed. Bud worked on his emails as he played catch up, and I grabbed a book, thinking it would help me fall asleep.

Later, as my eyelids drooped, I laid my head on my pillow, willing sleep to take over. After several hours of sound sleep, something jolted me awake. I listened for sounds and heard nothing. But Maddox's smile, along with his hair and eyes, appeared in my mind. How can I forget about him and concentrate on my relationship with Bud? My feelings for Bud are real. Somehow, I need to let Maddox go.

Since sleep wouldn't return, I climbed from the bed and walked into the kitchen. I grabbed a glass of milk and stared out the kitchen window as I drank it. Then something flashed as a movement caught my eye. "Bud," I yelled.

Moments later, he padded into the kitchen. "There's someone out there." I pointed to the backyard. Bud walked over to the window and peered outside, seeing nothing.

"Jada, I see nothing. But I'll dress and look around. Stay here." Bud disappeared down the hallway. He returned wearing jeans and a black t-shirt. On the way out the back door, he slipped his gun from his holster and carried it at thigh level.

Waiting for Bud to return was nothing short of nerve-wracking. I couldn't see anything at the back of the lot. Did I imagine seeing movement? No, something flashed, but what was it?

Bud walked through the back door empty-handed. "I saw nothing, Jada. It's so dark out there. I couldn't tell if there were footprints. I can check on it in the morning. Come on. We need you to rest." Bud reached out, taking my hand, leading me back to bed. He climbed in beside me, and I snuggled up to him. Being in his arms makes everything better, and dreamless sleep returned.

The alarm blared, and it startled me. Because I forgot what it sounded like or because I remained in my safe place. Bud chuckled. "Don't laugh. That thing scared me too. I'll start the coffee, and it'll be ready after your shower." I walked off to the kitchen feeling foolish. Today was my first day back at the office since my injury. I'm eager to return and catch up on the Augustus case.

Bud drove me to the office since I can't drive myself yet. He and Ivey have a meeting today with the FBI to discuss their status. Ivey says she's ready to take fresh cases, but I don't want them leaving town. I need them here with me.

Everyone greeted me at the door. Maggie was front and center. She hugged me and gave me a cup of coffee. She knows me too well. After the greeting, I entered my office. Everything remained as if I had just stepped away for a minute. Augustus' picture stared back at me, making my body tingle with rage. Why haven't we captured him yet?

Augustus reminded me that Taylor and Maddox are driving to Jackson this morning. I hope the trip helped us find this guy because if Lyle helped Augustus escape, he might know where he's hiding. Taylor mentioned Augustus and his guys never returned to the campsite where the agents suffered injuries.

I found my notebook and opened it to the last page, where I jotted notes from Taylor's updates. Ivey will follow up on the video enhancements, and Doc James will call today with the burned victim's identity.

Several papers were in my inbox, so I started there, then moved on to my email. It's incredible how far you can get behind in a short amount of time. Lucky for me, I'm a fast worker, and by lunchtime, I was back on track. Then I wondered why Taylor hadn't called.

As I stood from my desk, Bud and Ivey appeared in the doorway. "We are your lunch dates. Are you ready?" Bud asked.

"Yes, I'm ready. I can't believe it's lunch already as I've been nonstop since I arrived, but things are in order, thanks to Taylor." I said as I looked at Ivey. She beamed.

Lunch went by fast, but all I thought of was finding Augustus. I wanted that part of my life behind bars. How could no one find him? I wanted to review the old file we had on him. As the group entered the side of the Sheriff's Office, my cellphone rang.

"Hey, Taylor. Is everything okay? You what? Hold on. Ivey and Bud are with me. I'll put the phone on speaker so we can hear the outcome." I waved Ivey and Bud into my office, placing the phone on the desk. "Ok. Taylor. Tell us what happened."

"Are you ready? This is unbelievable. Maddox and I drove up to Lyle's house and parked behind his loaded SUV. When we knocked on the door, a younger woman answered the door, and we assumed she was Lyle's wife. But instead, she turned out to be Lyle's sister, who is married to Augustus."

Chapter 15

"Wait, a second. Did you say Augustus is married?" I asked.

"Yes, I did. Lyle's sister, Simone, married Augustus not long after high school. When Augustus went to prison, she moved in with Lyle. While we looked like fools, she thought everyone knew they had married. Lyle was in the shower when we first arrived, so we chatted with Augustus' wife. She claims to have no idea where he's hiding, which worries her. The escape caught her by surprise, too. We asked if Lyle had extracurricular activities, and she says he carries two cell phones and is constantly on them."

I didn't comment because it took a minute to process the information. "We found out Augustus married Lyle's sister. Lyle is a corrections officer living above his means. He carries two cell phones and appears to have heavy usage of them."

Bud shakes his head and says, "that's amazing, but how did Augustus keep his marriage a secret, and why?"

"We can't answer that yet, Bud. When Lyle met us in the family room, he stopped short. We introduced ourselves and started asking questions about Augustus. As soon as we hinted about his involvement in the escape, he stopped talking and requested we speak with his attorney. On our way out the door, we left business cards on the table for Lyle and handed a set to Augustus' wife."

"She won't call. Lyle won't give her the option. Did anyone pull Lyle's financials?" I inquired.

This time Maddox spoke. "We have them here with us. His financials are interesting, with cash deposits just under the reporting limits. We'll bring them back to you for your records. This guy is dirty, but we haven't put it all together yet. We should be back at the office in two hours."

"I'll be here when you arrive," I stated. When I raised my eyes, Bud stared back at me.

"Cash deposits usually mean one thing—illegal business enterprise. If Lyle had a criminal background, the state prison wouldn't have hired him. So, why now?" Bud asked as his head swiveled from me to Ivey.

I looked at the board and the information added over the last week. Augustus was a big-time drug dealer when he murdered his friend. That's why he wanted the winnings so badly. He needed the cash to buy more dope. "Do you think Augustus continued his drug enterprise inside the prison, using Lyle as the middleman?"

Ivey and Bud agreed. "That is the most plausible explanation yet. Taylor said Lyle's house and vehicle were out of his financial means on a corrections officer's salary. How else would he come up with all that money?"

Bud continued, "if Lyle made cash deposits, there would be no way of tracing the money. Does Augustus still have an open account anywhere?"

"We didn't find one in town. But we didn't know he was married either. When the guys return, we'll get her name and ask for her financials. She may hold the funds." I stated. As more ideas popped into my mind, I wrote them down. We couldn't afford to overlook anything.

Ivey's phone rings, and she points to the caller ID. "It's our call, Bud. We'll step out while we speak with an Atlanta Agent. Let us know when the guys arrive."

I nodded and sucked in a breath. I couldn't decide if I was eager to see Maddox or the information they gathered on Augustus or both. The marriage was a surprise. No one mentioned it during the trial. Was Augustus trying to protect her, and if so, from whom? Who was she before she married Augustus?

Two hours later, a window reflection passed before me, and I watched Maddox pull into the space in front of my window. I readied myself for the inevitable. Since Augustus remained on the run, Maddox was a fixture. As soon as they capture Augustus and his guys, Maddox will travel to another town in another state and start the chase again.

Once I discovered that revelation, I could face Maddox without fear until Maddox walked through my office door. As soon as we made eye contact, I couldn't remember my earlier revelation. My brain turned to mush, but I recovered when I noticed Taylor and Bud staring at me.

The office tension was noticeable, and when Ivey entered, she helped soften it by asking us to move to the conference room. She glared at me, too, but I didn't acknowledge her. I gathered my notes and walked to the conference room. Maddox trailed behind me, and I could feel his eyes roving over my body, but I dared not turn around. Bud spoke to me, but I heard nothing.

I plopped down in the first seat I came upon because I thought it was safe. Bud took one side while Ivey took the other. That left Maddox and Taylor sitting opposite of us. Maddox chose the seat directly in front of me while Taylor took the next one.

Bud cleared his throat and said, "where are the financials? We want to look at those as soon as possible. The techs called Ivey earlier, and they should have the video enhancements wrapped up shortly. They seem to think the results will please us."

"Do you think they found something useful in the pictures?" I directed my question to Ivey.

"The caller said they would highlight the areas of interest. Other than that, not much else," Ivey explained.

Maddox and Taylor unpacked their information while the others discussed the videos. Then, the guys separated the bank statements placing them on the table to show their findings. Bud leaned over the table and mumbled to himself.

"What did you find, Bud?" I asked because I was curious about what he found so quickly.

"Look at this." Bud pointed to last month's bank statement. "Lyle tried to be smart, but it didn't work out. His deposits were in different amounts but under the suspicious activity reporting figure. Some deposits were $9998, $9995, and so on. Did he not think someone would spot those amounts and question them?"

"I'm impressed, Bud. It took you three seconds to find it. Now, look at the other bank statements. We have statements from the last twenty-four months containing the same type of deposits. We're talking over a million dollars. Where do you suppose a prison guard gets his hands on that much money?" Maddox looked around the table, waiting for an answer.

"Drugs." Everyone said in unison, chuckling.

Taylor stated, "Maddox requested Augustus' wife's financials, but those won't be available until tomorrow. So, everyone, take whatever time you need to peruse the documents. Take notes of those items needing follow-up. I'm stepping out for coffee. Can I bring anyone one?"

Hands flew into the air, and then everyone snickered. Taylor shook his head because he knew how everyone loved their coffee. Maddox followed him out of the office. But not before he turned to

194

glimpse me. I felt his eyes on me, but I kept mine on the paper, especially since Bud watched the exchange.

A few minutes went by before Taylor and Maddox returned. Maddox held another box of paper while Taylor brought the coffee to us in a box top. "Now that you're back. Who wants to describe Lyle's house? I'm curious what it must be like." I asked.

Taylor and Maddox exchanged glances, with Taylor taking the lead. "It's stucco and stone, with a massive front porch. The house boasts a foyer the size of this room, and we walked through it to the family room. That room had a floor-to-ceiling window on one wall and a fireplace on the other. The kitchen would make a chef do a double-take. They have the biggest refrigerator I've ever seen." Taylor played with his phone until he found the picture. "Here, this is the only picture I took while we were there."

All eyes turned to the picture with oohs and ah's around the table. Ivey said, "that's too big. No one needs that much space."

"Unless you have multiple families living with you. Augustus's wife answered the door, and it sounded like she had come from upstairs. So, we assumed there was a primary suite somewhere on the first floor, and the others stayed upstairs. We saw no children. Just those two were in the house." Maddox added. "The view to the backyard was spectacular. Whoever manicures Lyle's lawn deserves a promotion because that yard was spotless."

195

Something spurred me to ask for a calendar. Taylor opened one of his phones. "What is it, Sheriff?"

"Give me a second," I asked, then went to work. I checked the dates of the deposits. "Lyle makes his deposits on Fridays or Mondays, sometimes in the same week. If he's running drugs, that makes sense. Is there chatter on the streets about a big drug deal happening? That could be the reason Augustus escaped. Lyle needed him on the outside to make it happen."

Everyone at the table grew silent as they pondered my observation. Taylor spoke first. "I haven't heard of one, but I haven't been on the streets lately either. Let's check with the other deputies. They can reach out to their informants too."

"Ok. Make it happen, Taylor." I instructed. Taylor stroked a note in his notebook for later.

Then Maddox joined the conversation. "do you have a list of friends Augustus hung out with other than Duke and Jermaine?"

"If I remember, there were four or five, I think. But one died last year. He had a small group of friends, even in school. I can get it for you." I leaned over my chair and plucked a file out of my stack. After thumbing through the papers, I found what I needed. "Here you go. Just make a copy."

"Thanks, Sheriff. One other note here, two agents are sitting on Lyle. They have instructions to follow him and photograph anyone he speaks with outside the home. It was obvious we rattled him today. I'm hoping he leads us to Augustus." Maddox shared.

"Did you mention the two cell phones, Maddox?" Taylor asked.

"No, I didn't. That information is on the back of the page. I wasn't there yet. Augustus' wife, Simone, shared that Lyle carries two cell phones and uses them constantly. She acted oblivious to our questions. Simone wanted to know when Augustus was getting out of prison for good." Taylor chuckled because once they captured Augustus, he would die in prison as an older man before the prison system would parole him.

No one commented on Taylor's information. Each person thought through the information received today, and no one had an answer, only more questions. "Who needs two cell phones? Does he use one for personal and one for the prison?" I inquired.

"That's easy enough to find out," Maddox stated as he picked his phone up from the table. He swiped upward and tapped the button for the prison warden. He answered on the second ring. Maddox explained what he needed, and within seconds, he had his answer.

"The prison doesn't supply cell phones to its guards. Instead, they use radios while at work." Maddox stated as he looked around the table.

Bud offered to get a warrant on Lyle's known phone number. So, Taylor passed the number to him, and he stepped out of the room to make his case to the tech investigator. As he left, my phone sounded.

I answered Doc James' call. Then I turned her speaker on so the group could hear the news, too. "The burned victim is Wilbur Jurgens, age 62. His address is off Rt 3. He works at the power plant down the road from the bar where we found him. The county shows he's the registered owner of a 2010 Chevrolet Tahoe and a 2015 Cadillac."

"Thanks, Doc. I'll send some guys to the residence for a welfare check. We'll be in touch." I stated. Why kill a 62-year-old man? Was it for his truck?

I collected myself. Then I called Tuttle because I wanted him and Johnson to handle the welfare check on Mr. Jurgens.

Tuttle stuttered, "Wilbur Jurgens, Sheriff?"

"Yes, why? Do you know him?" I questioned Tuttle as I made eye contact with Ivey and Taylor because Tuttle's voice concerned me.

"Mrs. Jurgens is sitting at Johnson's desk filling out a missing person report for her husband right now."

"I'm on my way," I answered Tuttle, looking at Ivey, Taylor, and Maddox. "Mrs. Jurgens is filling out a missing person report on her husband in Johnson's office. I'm going to break the news to her." I stood and straightened out my uniform, fixed my ponytail, and walked out the conference room door with my head held high and my shoulders back.

When I rounded the corner and spotted Mrs. Jurgens, my heart fluttered. How hard would it be to live so long and then, in a puff, your life partner snuffed out in a flash? Life isn't fair. I touched Mrs. Jurgens on the shoulder. When she saw me, she knew why I was there.

I walked her to a small alcove in the bullpen and told her the news. It shocked her to the core. She crumbled in my arms, and I yelled for help. Mrs. Jurgens wasn't a petite lady, and with her being dead weight, I couldn't hold on to her. Tuttle and Johnson rushed to my aid and quickly took over. They picked her up and carried her to the sofa in my office.

While they did that, I called for an ambulance. "Do you think she fainted?" I asked the guys because I hoped it wasn't any more serious than that.

"I feel a pulse, and she's breathing, so I guess she fainted," Johnson added as he stared at her lifeless form.

Bud came around the corner and ran into me. "Sorry. You didn't return, and I got nervous. Who's that?" Bud asked as he pointed to Mrs. Jurgens. Since he missed Doc James's call, I revisited the information from the Doc. "Poor lady. Maybe the EMTs can wake her up enough for an emergency contact number. Someone needs to be with her."

The EMTs rushed into my office and started checking her vitals. One EMT rubbed his balled fist into her chest, and she moaned. "She responded to pain stimuli." He unzipped a medical bag and broke open some smelling salts. As soon as he placed the pouch under her nose, she coughed.

She tried sitting up on the sofa but had difficulty. The EMT laid her back down as he checked her heart rate. "Now, we have elevated blood pressure. We need to get her to the hospital."

"Wait. Can I talk to her? I need to find out if there is a friend or family member that I can call for her." I begged.

The EMT nodded. "Mrs. Jurgens, do you have a family member or friend I can call for you?" She nodded.

"My daughter lives up in Canton. Can you call her? Her number is in my cell phone in my purse." Mrs. Jurgens said in a feeble voice.

Johnson found her purse on the floor, where she dropped it in my arms. He handed it to her. She reached inside a pocket and brought out her cell phone. Thumbing through her favorite list, she found the number. "I can't tell my daughter that someone murdered her dad." Then she reached up and wiped the tears that streamed from her eyes.

I jotted the number on my pad and watched as the EMTs loaded Mrs. Jurgens onto a stretcher. I whispered in an EMT's ear that I would notify the daughter and let the hospital know.

That ordeal drained me. I sat in my chair with my elbows propped on my desk and my head in my hands. How much more death will Augustus inflict on my county? Rage bubbled closer to the surface at every turn.

Bud had stepped away during Mrs. Jurgens's removal, but he rejoined me with a mug full of hot coffee. I sighed. "Thanks, Bud. Now, for another death notification. I hope this girl holds it together for her mother."

"She will. She'll be the rock Mrs. Jurgens needs."

I picked up the telephone and dialed the number for the Jurgens' daughter. She answered on the second ring. As soon as I identified myself, she turned silent. I stated my business and waited for a reply. It took several seconds for the news to sink in, but when it did, she said, "I'm on my way. I'll go straight to the hospital. Thanks for calling Sheriff."

After giving her my cell phone number, our call ended, and I sucked in a deep breath as my nerves calmed. I wrote myself a note to stop by the hospital on my way home.

Bud had the phone to his ear when I turned my attention to him. From Bud's expression, it appears to be more bad news. I'm not sure if I can take any more news today. With the Jurgens on my mind, Louisa popped in, too. That reminded me to check on her tonight at the hospital. If she wakes from her coma and identifies Micah as the driver, he won't be getting out of prison soon.

I watched Bud end the call and looked at the murder board. His shoulders sagged as he revisited the phone conversation. "That was the lab tech working on our lip reading. He admitted difficulty with our video, so he requested a second opinion before sharing what Augustus said in the video. I begged for whatever information he had, but he refused to give it to me."

So, I sat back in my chair, waiting for the results again. Unfortunately, this case has been nothing but a waiting game. We are waiting on Augustus' sketch results from the lab tech, and we still haven't received the enhanced photos yet.

A thought jolted me to action. I jumped up from my desk and ran into the parking lot. There sat a 2015 Cadillac. Now, I know what vehicle Augustus is driving.

Chapter 16

Bud stood at the side door of the office, staring at me. "What are you doing?"

"I just remembered Mrs. Jurgens drove herself to the office to file a report. Wilbur has two vehicles registered with him. If she drives the Cadillac, chances are he drives the Tahoe." I smiled when Bud followed my process.

"Sheriff, you're amazing. Here my mind is on the lip-reading, and while you're thinking of something else, this popped into your mind. You're a real multi-tasker." Bud pecked me on the cheek as I crossed the threshold.

"I need to get a BOLO issued on the Tahoe. So, I'll be right back." I jogged to dispatch and spoke with Sgt T. She agreed to handle my request pronto. As I walked away, I heard her call all cars and announce the BOLO for Jurgen's 2010 Tahoe. I smiled while I whispered a prayer for us to find it before Augustus and his boys killed someone else.

On my way to the conference room, I stopped in my office to ensure nothing was waiting for me, and it wasn't. So I continued to the conference room. Everyone sat around staring at each other, deciding on our next step.

Ivey alerted us to the information from Maddox's contact. Ivey instructed Maddox to share his findings.

"I received an email concerning the financials. Augustus's name wasn't on an account alone. He shares one with Simone Fins. It looks like it holds enough money for monthly bills and a little spending money for Simone. There is no record of money leaving the account for rent or utilities. We assume Lyle lets her stay at his house rent-free. The search continues for more accounts. If Lyle and Augustus are in this together, there are more accounts somewhere. I wondered if greed took over and Lyle deposited the funds without Augustus' consent."

We chuckled. "That would be a sight to see. Augustus found out Lyle double-crossed him. I want to be there for that show." Taylor laughed. "Lyle won't be able to run far enough away to escape Augustus."

I called Sgt T and asked for an update on the BOLO for the Tahoe. With no sightings, I asked Bud to accompany me to the hospital. Mrs. Jurgens should be in a room by now, and I wanted to see if she was resting.

We bid goodbyes to the group, and my eyes lingered on Maddox a little longer than they should have. He didn't wink or move. We just enjoyed the view.

Bud never mentioned the eye contact, and neither did I. We discussed the case on the ride to the hospital, with Augustus being the number one topic. We threw ideas back and forth about a potential hiding place and decided Augustus and his guys were probably hiding by the river. With the river being miles long, there is no way to walk in and find them without air support.

However, Bud explained air support is only as good as the ground they cover. If the trees touch one another, it would be less likely the air patrol would spot the escapee. They can use infrared camera capability, but it will also pick up animal heat signatures, leaving the ground support in an unknown situation.

At every turn, I felt I had to take two steps back. Why couldn't we get ahead of this guy? Now, I wondered if he's even in my county? Just because he murdered people in my county didn't mean he was hiding here.

Bud took my elbow and ushered me inside the hospital. He has remained on edge since my encounter at the kitchen window. We feel like someone is watching us, but neither has spotted the culprit. We walked to the information desk, and the lady provided Mrs. Jurgens' room number.

We waved off the map and headed to the elevator. When the doors opened, we sidestepped to allow a passenger to pass between us. I walked into Mrs. Jurgens's room first, then Bud followed.

"Hi. Mrs. Jurgens. May I come inside?" I asked because she appeared asleep, and I felt terrible about disturbing her.

"Yes. Please do."

Bud trailed behind me, and as I walked to the bed, Mrs. Jurgens readjusted herself. "How are you feeling? You sure gave us a scare." I stated as I grinned at her.

"Much better. The doctors and nurses have been so nice to me. They keep checking on me every thirty minutes. They say I'll be here until tomorrow afternoon. The doctor wants to make sure I don't have another episode. Plus, my daughter is arriving in a few hours. Thank you for calling her." Mrs. Jurgen expressed her thanks while wiping a tear as it trickled down her cheek.

"You're welcome, Mrs. Jurgens. Is there anything I can get for you?" I looked around the room. It was bare.

"No, Sheriff. I'm fine." Mrs. Jurgens patted my hand as I rested it on her arm.

"Well, we'll be on our way. Please call me if you need anything. Let me know when your daughter arrives. She has my number." Mrs. Jurgens nodded, and with that, Bud and I exited the room.

Once the elevator doors closed, Bud stated, "she is one tough lady. She kept a smile on her face throughout our visit." Bud shook his head in amazement. One floor down, we stepped off onto another floor. This stop I somewhat dreaded. I felt terrible for Louisa and her family, but I couldn't make her well.

When we turned the corner, we heard someone speaking in rapid-fire Spanish. Louisa's mom spotted us first. "Sheriff." She called and waved for us to stop. I grinned when I realized she was a Spanish speaker.

"Sheriff. Louisa is awake. I'm so excited that I've been calling family. Come. Come this way, and you can see for yourself." I glanced at Bud, and he nodded. We followed.

We entered yet another hospital room. Louisa sat up in bed, propped up on a mound of pillows. Some of her injuries were healing, while others remained wrapped in bandages. I noticed the doctors reattached her ear, and thank goodness, they covered it.

Bud stayed closer to the door, and I walked over to Louisa. "Hi. Louisa. Your mom told us you were awake. I'm glad you're on the mend."

"Thanks, Sheriff, for finding me. My parents told me you and a deputy found me on the road. Did you get the guy who did this to me?" Louisa questioned with a steadfast determination.

"Deputy Taylor and I found you in the street after an anonymous call to 911. We arrested Micah Sutter, but it would go a long way with the court if you identified him. Would you try it if I brought by a photo lineup later?"

"Yes, please do that. I'll never forget his face. When I get out of here, I want to be in the courtroom when they sentence him to life in prison." A lone tear slid down her cheek as she made her statement.

"I'll make it happen within the next two days. Rest today, and then we'll make plans for the photo lineup." I smiled, turned, and shook hands with her parents on our way out the door.

We didn't speak until we were safely inside the elevator. "I can't believe she looks that good. When we found her, I didn't expect her to make it through the night, let alone wake up and tell me she wants a photo lineup."

"If you ask me, she is fortunate you and Taylor followed through and scanned the length of the road. If you hadn't, she wouldn't be here today." Bud stated.

With Louisa awake and talking, she made my day. I couldn't wait to share the news with Taylor. We discussed the possibility of her not making it through the night.

"Do you feel like grabbing a bite before heading home?" I asked.

"Sure, if patrons pack the restaurant, we can sit in the back." Bud winked at me. Until we captured Augustus, there would be no sitting at the restaurant windows. I chuckled.

We chatted over supper about Bud's workload now that Ivey is back. They expected a fresh case any day, and who knows where it would take them? I cringed because that would leave me alone, and now that I have Bud and Ivey, I'm not willing to be alone. Bud saw the change in my eyes.

"Jada, you know it will be temporary, and yes, I'm coming home to you. I've told you before. This is home now and forever." As he said it, my eyes filled with tears. Again, I blinked them away in record time, and Bud chuckled.

"I'm sorry I did that, but I couldn't stop them. I guess with Augustus being on the run, I'm jumpy." I looked down because I didn't want my eyes to fill up again.

Bud reached over the table and took my hand. "Jada, Augustus will not win this chase. People are human, making mistakes, just like our last serial killer. Someone will spot Augustus or one of his guys in town, and we'll be there." Just as Bud finished, my cell phone dinged with a text message.

"It's Braxton. He wants me to call him. I'll let him know it will be a few minutes." I fired off the text, and we finished our meal. Then we headed to the car. Bud deposited me into the passenger seat while he slid under the wheel. By the time he started the car, I was on the phone with Deputy Braxton Long.

"Hey, Long, It's Sheriff Steele. What can I do for you?" I sat back and listened to Long tell me about a friend who overheard a conversation about a massive drug deal going down. It's supposed to happen within the next week, but there was no precise date or time.

"Long, keep working on this guy. Maybe he can lead us to someone else that might have more information. That's great work. Thanks, Long."

"Long might have tipped the iceberg in our favor," I repeated Long's conversation to Bud and watched Bud's eyebrows bunch together as he worked through the information. "What's with the look, Bud?"

"A massive drug deal. That's the words Long used?" Bud asked.

I nodded and waited. Then Bud said, "that sounds like something that would interest the FBI if it turned out as big as this guy said. Do you care if I make a few phone calls? It might help us narrow down a search area."

"Go for it. I'll take all the help I can get. But right now, I'm tired. Take me home."

Bud's face broke out into a grin, reaching ear to ear. "I like the sound of that." Then darkness fell as they drove home. Several times, I watched Bud study the rearview mirror but didn't ask questions. Mainly because Bud would have spoken up if there was a problem and the other reason was I just didn't want to know.

As I lay in bed, I wondered about my injury. Somehow, I don't feel like myself. Sometimes I feel like I am floating along, then my head pounds for a few minutes, and finally, it subsides. No one knows because I don't want to spend more time in the hospital. So until Augustus is behind bars, I'm not mentioning my symptoms, but I'll see my doctor again when we capture him. Maybe the blow to my head jarred something loose. With that thought, I rolled over and fell into a deep sleep.

One dream after another invaded my mind. One minute I ran from someone, and then another, I ran after someone else. Both times, it was only a shadow. I never saw faces, and I was always alone. Finally, toward daybreak, I woke up soaking wet with sweat. Apparently, I screamed out in my sleep because Bud came running.

The door flew open, hitting the wall behind it. "Jada, are you okay?" Bud placed his knee on the bed beside me and wrapped me in his arms. He didn't care if sweat drenched me.

I snuggled into his arms as I tried to remember my dreams. "I'm okay. I guess it was a dream, but I can't remember much. It must have been a doozy since I am drenched. I'm sorry for screaming or whatever I did."

"When you screamed, it curdled my blood. I thought someone was attacking you." Bud's voice was tense.

"It's weird having such a powerful dream than not being able to remember it. I'll take a shower since there is no way for me to go back to sleep now. Why don't you try to get some more sleep? I promise I'll be quiet." I rubbed Bud's face and placed a kiss on his lips.

"Sit here with me a minute, Jada. I can't stop hearing that scream." I laid my head on his chest, and with the feeling of safety, we drifted off to sleep. We woke a few hours later to my alarm blaring.

"Thanks, Bud, for your comfort. Those last few hours of sleep were the best I've had in a long time." I shared. But I kept my sleep troubles to myself for now.

Bud made coffee and a bagel for me while I showered. When I opened the bathroom door, the coffee aroma stirred my senses. Then the bagel. I didn't think this day could get any better.

We made it to the office without incident, and I felt better than I had in days. "Sheriff, you have packages on your desk," Maggie stated with a grin.

I walked into my office without stopping at Maggie's desk because I wanted to see the packages. I leaned out the door, "Bud, it's the enhanced photos."

Bud trotted into my office and grabbed a tube since mailing tubes covered my desk. We started unrolling the photos when Ivey and Taylor stopped in to say hello. We put them to work too. After all the photos lay flat on the table, we looked at each other. Now what?

"How about taping these pictures to the conference room walls and sorting the enlarged ones? We don't have enough wall space for these pictures." I suggested.

Ivey added, "I'll sort the enlarged quadrants matching the original photo. Maybe if we inspect the larger photos first, then if we spot something of interest, we can find the match and use those." Ivey looked at us, waiting for a reply.

Taylor answered. "Let's do it. If it doesn't work, we'll try something else."

"I've got the tape dispenser from Jada's desk. Maybe Maggie can help too." Bud offered.

We exited my office with our hands loaded with pictures. I stopped by Maggie's desk and asked her for her help on our way. She obliged, finding another tape dispenser for us. Then we ran into Tuttle and Long on the way to the conference room. They offered their services too. With so many helpers, it didn't take long to tape the forty pictures to the wall.

As I stood in the room, excitement coursed through my veins. My answers are in these pictures. We just have to find them. If I were using pictures to communicate, where and how would I hide them?

I glanced over at the landscapes. They were consistent in that each picture had a river with rocks and trees. The sun shone in several, while others boasted a cloudy sky. Would Augustus use the water or maybe raindrops to conceal information? I walked over to a picture, studied the raindrops, and saw nothing of interest.

"Study the pictures and let me know if you notice anything interesting. Be diligent. Whatever is in these pictures, the naked eye won't notice it." I instructed.

Over the next two hours, we walked into the room, took notes, studied a few of the enlarged photos, then I sat down and stared at the walls. Unfortunately, Taylor, Long, and Tuttle had long since gone on patrol. That left me, Bud, and Ivey to study the pictures. Maggie escaped the picture detail too.

This process frustrated me. I'm not an artist, so I'm unsure how someone can hide answers in a picture. Then I heard, "codes. People have hidden coded words in pictures." Bud whispered to himself as he worked through his idea.

"What did you say, Bud? We couldn't hear you." Ivey asked as I looked on, too.

"There might be a code in these pictures, not words, but a code. The code can lead to words. We must find the code first, and then the FBI can translate the code into words." Bud explained.

"Ok. I like it. What should I look for?" I asked as I studied a picture.

"That's the hard part, as I can't answer. Over the years, I've worked on cases involving codes. Some were complicated, but we used a computer program to solve the question. The others were easy to solve with pen and paper. We'll have to find it before I can give you a precise answer."

Maggie entered the room with a bag from the nearest office supply store. "Here, these might come in handy." She reached inside the bag and handed each of us a magnifying glass. We laughed.

"You're right, Maggie. These will help us find the code. I hope you bought enough for everyone to help." I stated, then tried one out on a picture. "Oh, this was a brilliant idea, Maggie. This helps us see the smallest detail."

Bud stepped out of the room and answered a call while playing with the magnifying glasses. I found slash marks I thought were in a strange place, but nothing else stood out as odd in that picture. So I placed a hot pink sticker on the slash marks.

"Whoa. Augustus is a bona fide artist. It's too bad he didn't use his talents for a legitimate business instead of a criminal one." Taylor expressed as he walked around the room, studying each picture.

Bud rejoined the group as Long followed him into the room. The pictures shocked Long, too, just as they had the rest of us. Bud explained his call to the Atlanta FBI office and saw Ivey's expression. He held his hand up. "wait, Ivey and Taylor, you don't know about our conversation with Long. Deputy, will share with the team?"

Chapter 17

Deputy Long shared the same information with Ivey and Taylor that he did with us. He has learned nothing new about a drug deal. Taylor jumped on the news, letting us know he has a confidential informant he has used in the past for drug deals. Everyone nodded and asked him to follow up on it. He slipped out of the room.

I stood and stretched. We've been in this room for hours, and I needed a break. "It's time for lunch. Let's take a break, and we can pick this up later." I walked out of the room and headed to my office. Bud followed. We passed Taylor as he spoke on his phone. He jotted notes.

Bud saw this too and whispered, "I hope he gets us something."

"Me too. Help me remember to share Louisa's status. I haven't told him yet. I also need a photo lineup for her. So, I'll have Captain Grayson handle the lineup for me, but I wanted to meet with Louisa. I wanted to see how quickly she identifies this guy."

As soon as I sat behind my desk, Taylor entered, saying, "We have another person confirming a massive drug deal. But unfortunately, he was unsure where or when they planned to do it. He will call me when he hears anything."

"Sounds good to me, Taylor. Let us know. I forgot to share about Louisa. She's awake and looks good compared to when we found her. Bud and I visited her last night after stopping in on Mrs. Jurgens. Louisa agreed to a photo lineup. I'll have Captain Grayson make one up for us since we are neck-deep in finding Augustus, and then I'll stop in and see her."

"I can't believe she is doing so well. She's a strong girl to endure that much bodily damage and agree to a photo lineup so soon." Taylor exclaimed.

As Taylor exited, I picked up my phone and summoned Captain Grayson. While I waited for him to trek through the Sheriff's Office, I pondered the pictures. Would Augustus have one message in each picture, or would each picture have a word to form a sentence? If it's the last one, we have no idea which order they delivered these pictures without viewing the videos again, which will take hours.

Captain Grayson entered my office in a huff. I looked up at him and smiled. He never gets upset, and when he does, his face turns beet red. "What's up, Captain?"

"We have an unruly inmate. Nothing I can't handle in time. Which prisoner do I include in this photo lineup?" He removed his pen from his shirt pocket and placed it on his pad.

"Micah Sutter. The victim from the car race is awake and volunteered to look at a photo lineup since she will stay in the hospital for a while. If she picks him out of six guys, we have him, and he

217

won't be getting out of jail in the foreseeable future. We can't pin him with Aidan's murder until the DNA test comes back from the lab."

"Are you sure it's Micah? He's the troublemaker. He shouts at the top of his lungs about his innocence and how we violated all kinds of laws." Captain Grayson shared.

"Did he call for his attorney?"

Captain Grayson shook his head and stated, "he has no money, so he'll get a public defender."

"Swell. We can move him through the system once Louisa identifies him. Put him in solitary if he doesn't cooperate." I instructed.

"Where do you think he is? That's what I was doing when you called." Grayson snickered. "Micah thinks he's above the law. He keeps saying he knows something, but what that is, I don't have a clue. He doesn't like me. So, he isn't talking."

"Thanks for the information, Grayson. Get me the photo lineup as soon as you can. Then I might pop over and visit with Micah. If he knows Louisa identified him, he might be willing to talk." Grayson left my office, and I wondered what Micah referenced in his rants.

Bud poked his head into my office, "Can you break for lunch? I'm starving."

"Now works for me, too." I gathered my keys and walked to meet Bud at the side door when the radio crackled in my hand. I shrugged my shoulders as I glanced at Bud.

A half-second later, the radio came to life. "Sheriff Maddox received notice of an Augustus sighting. He requested backup."

"Send it over the radio. Show me en route, too." I jogged to my car with Bud right on my heels. "Bud, I can meet you if you want to grab lunch."

"No way. I'm riding with you. If Maddox has Augustus, I want to witness the takedown." Bud shared. He slid into the car and buckled his seatbelt before I started the car.

As I pulled out of the lot, dispatch conveyed Maddox's whereabouts, and I gunned it. A passerby spotted Duke driving Mr. Jurgens Tahoe on Rt 3 toward the river. It was lunchtime, and I needed to be on the other side of town. I flipped the controls for the lights and sirens and headed to Rt 3. Taylor, Tuttle, and Long radioed the same.

Traffic wasn't on my side today. I swerved into a right-turn-only lane and hopped onto a side street that ran parallel to the town's main street. Once we cleared the town, the roads opened, and we flew to Rt 3. Before we made it, a GSP officer spotted it heading toward the interstate.

"Something is up with Duke and Augusts hitting the interstate. I remember Taylor saying something like this happened in his chase. Let's head toward the interstate. We might get lucky and meet him." I stated as I pressed the pedal a little closer to the floor.

Taylor and Tuttle were ahead of us, following the same path. Long was driving north on the interstate, which would have him following Duke. With one of us behind him and the rest heading straight for him, how can we miss?

I picked up the mic and asked for a status. Then I waited.

Each of my deputies reported to me that the Tahoe had vanished. Just like last time. I slammed my hand on the steering wheel, grimacing as pain radiated to my shoulder.

"Sheriff, we'll find him. What is the area where it vanishes?" Bud questioned as he looked at his surroundings.

"Just what you see out the window. Nothing. That's what's out here, nothing. Acres of undeveloped land and the river. I'll have Taylor check the satellite imagery of this area and see if he spots something."

I leaned over and picked the mic up, holding it to my mouth. "Deputy Taylor, report to the office. Maddox, call my cell."

With pain in my shoulder, I rubbed it, hoping it would subside. I completed a 180 on the road, turned my lights and sirens off, and returned to the office. Just as I reached out to open my door, Taylor backed into the space beside me.

"Sheriff. You wanted to see me." Taylor stated as he glanced at Bud.

"Yes. Can you work with the satellite imagery and tell me what is in that area off Rt 3? I'm looking for something that conceals a car and three men. There is a reason he keeps driving to that area, and I want to know what it is."

"10-4. I'll do it now." Taylor trotted off to the door. He glanced back, but he closed the door since we still stood in place.

Bud ran his fingers through his hair as he ran ideas through his head. My cell phone rang, and I snatched it up without checking the caller ID. My heart landed in my throat when I heard Maddox's raspy voice on the other end.

I had to remain professional through this ordeal, but with Maddox, that's a difficult feat. "Did you find anything, Maddox? We saw nothing. I have Taylor working his magic with the satellite imagery to see what he can find. It's a lot of ground to cover, so it will be awhile before we find it."

Maddox paused then said, "we have nothing, except my guys sitting on Lyle's house advised me off a late-night visitor. The person drove a flower delivery van, and he never faced my guy. So they couldn't identify the person if they had to."

"A flower delivery person in the middle of the night seems odd. Does Lyle know you're watching him?" I questioned.

"I don't see how. We secured a vacant house and are watching through plantation shutters. The guys never use lights when the sun goes down. If they leave, they use the road at the back of the house and never pass in front of Lyle's house."

"Does the girl ever leave?"

"No, Publix dropped off their groceries yesterday. I'm not sure what the girl does all day, but she hasn't left the house since we started our surveillance." Maddox explained.

"Ok. I wanted to let you know Augustus's pictures are in the conference room. You're welcome to drop by and look. They hold a clue, but we haven't found it yet."

"Thanks, Sheriff. I just might do that." Maddox said, then he ended the call.

I felt the air escape my lungs when our call ended. I still wasn't sure how I was supposed to think about Maddox. But when I turned my head, my eyes fell on Bud. He waved at me.

Walking to him, I could hear the excitement. He ended the call. "We have solid evidence of a drug deal. The FBI lip readers confirm the conversation where Augustus ran his fingers over his lips. Augustus told his visitor that the shipment was on its way, and the deal was in the works. One lip reader mentioned the word before shipment reads like heroin, but he is not 100% sure, so they left that out of their report."

"Fantastic news. We need to follow up with Long and Taylor. Maybe their snitches have heard something by now." I turned and headed into the office. Bud grabbed my arm and turned me to face him.

"I don't enjoy seeing you mad enough to slam the steering wheel. Don't hurt yourself over Augustus. He's not worth it." Bud leaned over and kissed my cheek.

"Thank you for the reminder, but I hate to lose. You know, for Augustus to slip through again is maddening. But with your information, we can turn our attention to drugs. Augustus is out for a drug deal. Now we must prove it. Our missing information is in the pictures." I stated with a new purpose. We opened the door and walked straight to the coffee bar, then to the conference room.

After I finished my coffee, my stomach growled. I glanced at Bud, and he stared at me. "Sounds like you are hungry. Want me to go grab something?"

"How about delivery? I'd rather stay here and work on the pictures. The pictures are a big key to this whole mess as they could hold the clues."

"I'll scrounge up something for lunch while you concentrate on the pictures." Bud offered.

I studied a picture that the lab had blown up for us with a magnifying glass in my hand. There were slash marks on the rocks, just like in the other picture, but one spot resembles the number 1. If there are numbers in these pictures, what does that tell me? Nothing other than they are using code to communicate.

I located the picture with my marker on it and used the glass again to inspect the slash marks. Sure enough, number one shows up at the end of the line. Are there other numbers hidden in these pictures? I continued scanning the picture, and I found the number nine. My pulse picked up as I contemplated my findings. Where is Bud? I need to show him what I found.

Captain Grayson entered the room, holding a file folder. "Sheriff, here is your photo lineup. I made it difficult because I wanted this guy to stay in prison for what he did. Let me know after you meet with the girl." He handed me the folder, and I opened it. It shocked me that all the guys in the photo's favor.

"This is great! Where did you find these photos?" I asked.

"Every one of these guys currently lives in your jail," Grayson said with a grin. "Which made the lineup easy."

"I'll schedule a time to meet with Louisa later today, and I'll let you know. Thanks, Grayson." I said as he left the room, waving at me over his head.

Bud returned, holding two salads and two travel cups full of sweet tea. I didn't know which I wanted more, the sweet tea or the salad. Either way, I accepted the gift. Over lunch, I explained my findings to Bud. Then he explained the code called

A1Z26, where each letter of the alphabet correlates with a number. He also described this code as easily breakable. His concern is Augustus might have used the code differently than intended. If so, it will be more difficult for us to decipher.

We dropped our empty salad containers in the trash and moved to the pictures. I handed Bud a magnifying glass and pointed out my find. He continued searching the picture for more numbers, finding more on another rock. "Look here, Jada, there are more numbers in this rock. I think he uses the rocks for his numbers. Let's take each picture and search the rocks. Write the numbers on paper and keep that paper with the pictures. We might need the pictures to help decipher the word."

"Let's try it. Should we try one together?" I questioned since I was unsure of the process. Working side by side with Bud would help me see the steps.

He agreed and plucked a picture from the stack. We sat beside each other, and I watched him scan the rocks. Once he found a number, he jotted it on paper and continued. After he inspected the picture, he found a series of numbers. He showed me the numbers, and I shrugged my shoulders. The numbers meant nothing to me. Now, we must match the numbers to letters and unscramble the letters to make a word.

With a blank piece of paper, we list the numbers, then the letters. We look at the letters for a second. Then both say ambulance. Thinking about our first word, "did Augustus work out his escape through the pictures? Remember, he used an illness to summon an ambulance for his escape."

"That's possible. Why else would he mention an ambulance?" Bud stated as he reached for another picture. He put the magnifying glass to the picture and searched the rocks. "I see nothing in this one. Why go to the trouble of drawing this if it didn't have a code inside?"

"Look at something besides the rocks. Could he use the water to hide the numbers?"

"Let me try the water. I thought about the tree trunks, too. Both would make good hiding places." Bud slid the glass up the page to the water. He scanned both sides of the river and came up empty-handed. "I see nothing in the water or on the tree trunk. There must be something here somewhere. I'm not giving up yet."

My cell phone rang. I answered Louisa's mom. She gave me the okay to meet Louisa around four since she spends the afternoon in physical therapy. I had high hopes for that meeting.

We plugged along hour after hour. Finally, as I prepared to leave for my visit with Louisa, Bud yelled, "I found it! The numbers are in the tree leaves. I'm going with you to see Louisa, and then we'll return here. We have more work to do." Bud's excitement was contagious.

With the file folder tucked under my arm, we exited the side door and stepped out into the late afternoon sun. "This sun is incredible. It causes such a glare on the chrome bumpers." I said as we walked to my car. I shielded my eyes to scan the parking lot because I stayed alert every time I stepped outside. There was no way to let Augustus get that close to me again without fighting.

Traffic was building as people got off work and headed home. Finally, we pulled into the hospital parking lot with five minutes to spare. "I'm eager to see Louisa's reaction. Since I'm banking on a good outcome, I brought sworn statements." We followed the hallway to Louisa's room, and I knocked gently on the door.

Louisa greeted us from the bed, so we entered, and I walked up to her bedside while Bud lingered at the door. I explained the process with the photo lineup. With her parents standing on the opposite side of the bed, I slid the lineup out of the folder. I laid it on top of the folder and held it out for all to view.

Fifteen seconds later, Louisa placed her finger square on Micah's face. Then she looked up at me, "please tell me you have this man in custody." Her eyes pleaded with me.

"Yes, Louisa, he's sitting in our jail. Thank you for this. I know it's hard looking at him again, but this seals his fate. Now, I have sworn statements I need you and one parent to sign, proving I did not coerce you in your selection."

Louisa and her dad signed the forms as tears rolled down Louisa's face. Her dad hugged her tight as he passed me the signed documents. I left them holding each other with a knot in my gut.

While Bud and I returned to the office, I planned my meeting with Micah. I was eager to meet him, as I wanted him to know I had proof of his actions. "Bud, I'm going to meet with Micah. I want him to know we have evidence proving he was the driver. He won't be getting out of jail for the foreseeable future."

"Ok. While you do that, I'll be in the conference room. I want to continue with our pictures." Bud said as he looked out the window.

Once we entered the building, I continued to the jail division, bypassing my office. Captain Grayson knew I was on my way to see him. He was just as eager as I. "I got it, Captain. Louisa picked Micah out within fifteen seconds of seeing the lineup. She showed no hesitation."

"That's great, Sheriff. Let me get Micah moved to an interview room." Grayson leaned over the counter, pressed a button, and uttered his directive. He escorted me to the room, and he followed me inside.

"You don't have to sit through this, Captain."

"I want to witness this. He has such a cocky attitude. This should drop him down a few notches." Grayson advised.

A deputy escorted a handcuffed Micah into the interview view. When Micah sat, the deputy removed the handcuffs, then cuffed him to a steel bar connected to the table. I sat across from him and noticed his smug expression.

Chapter 18

"Do you know why we're here, Micah?" I posed the question because I wanted to see his reaction.

"You know I have information, and you want it?" He gave me a crooked smile and waited. He thought he held the next play.

"Not exactly. I have a sworn statement from the girl you dragged across the pavement while driving your speeding car. I have charged you with attempted murder, and when the DNA tests come back from Aidan's murder, I will add murder to your growing list."

"Wait, what? This isn't about what I know." Micah asked with wide eyes.

"No, it's not. We're here to let you know you'll be our guest for a while, so get comfortable." I slid my chair back, showing Micah our meeting was over. Grayson followed.

"Sheriff, I have information for you, but we need an agreement." Micah squirmed in his way, but the restraints didn't give him the space he needed.

"I don't need to agree to anything. I've done my job, and that's finding you. If you have something to say, say it." I explained.

Micah stuttered as we caught him by surprise, but he regained his composure as he begged, "I want a deal. My information is newsworthy, but I'll be dead in a day if you don't protect me."

"I can't offer a deal, but I'll talk to the DA about keeping you off death row. You should see death row with what you did to that girl and Aidan's senseless murder." The longer I spoke, the wider Micah's eyes grew. From my tone, he finally grasped the seriousness of his situation.

Without another word, Captain Grayson and I exited the interview room. As soon as the door closed, Micah began screaming, "you need me. The sooner, the better!"

We continued down the corridor without a glance back. Finally, Captain Grayson inquired, "Sheriff, do you think he knows something?"

"Yes, I do. I think he knows about the upcoming drug deal involving Augustus. So I'm letting him sweat a little. I'll be back to meet again." I grinned as I explained my purpose.

Captain Grayson nodded in acknowledgment. He turned left at the intersection while I went right. My head spun as I tried to fit Micah into Augustus' situation. Do they know each other? That's my first question.

Since it was late in the day, I wanted to go home and think about anything but this case. Sometimes, the best idea is to step away when things get tough. Let other thoughts filter into your mind. Then it takes on a fresh look when you return to your situation.

When I entered the conference room, I didn't expect anyone other than Bud. "Hey, Ivey. I didn't know you would be here." I walked over and hugged her as she studied a picture. When I see her, I still can't believe we found each other after all these years.

"I'm working on this picture while Taylor is on the phone. I found more numbers in several areas in this picture." Ivey held up the picture she referenced. Then she handed me the numbers she had recorded on the paper.

"This is more than any I've found so far. First, we need to decipher the letters, then maybe the words will lead somewhere." I stated with excitement in my voice. Then I made a mental note to return to the other pictures and look at other areas besides the rocks.

Since Augustus scattered the numbers around the picture, he must have had a map uncovering the hidden letters. Do the letters flow left to right or right to left? Are they in a circle? With Ivey's find, we might shed some light on the code. If we can find a few words, it might lead us to the drug deal.

I turned to face the group. "I met with Louisa, and she identified Micah as the car driver. Then I met Micah and gave him the news. He told me he had information, but he needed protection and a deal. I left him with neither. I'll visit again tomorrow. Maybe he'll change his mind."

Taylor entered with worry lines stretched across his forehead. He nodded to the group, saying, "I've found nothing on the satellite maps. So far, it's been undeveloped land. But I scheduled a meeting tonight with my CI. The meeting is at midnight at our famous bar. Maybe he can offer us something on the drug deal." Taylor walked over and planted a kiss on Ivey's cheek. We watched her blush.

"Do you want back up, Taylor? I'm not sure you need to do this alone. I know you trust this guy, but I question the timing." He needed him to know I felt uneasy about this meeting. Midnight and at a bar. Why there?

Ivey interjected her thoughts. "I can ride with Taylor. I'll stay in the car while he meets his informant. The informant won't know I'm there." She stated as she stared at Taylor and me.

I paused before answering. Something niggled at my brain, but I couldn't say why. Was it because I met with Micah? I asked the guys to use their informants to find information on the drug deal, so why does this bother me? With no answers, I inspected Ivey's picture and the list she made of the number with the corresponding letters.

"This list doesn't form a word. It's primarily consonants. Either we missed numbers, or this doesn't belong in our code. Is this a phone number? I wrote the numbers on a new piece of paper straight across the top. It looked like I should know. There were too many numbers for a phone number. I added vowels between several letters as I tried to make this work. It didn't.

I continued working with the list Ivey provided me as she and Taylor stepped out for supper. Bud joined me and walked over to the table and studied my list. "What is that, Jada?"

"Ivey found these numbers in that picture." I pointed out the picture Ivey worked. "but the corresponding letters don't form words. I've tried adding vowels to make a word, but it doesn't work. It's strange. There are too many numbers for a phone number. What else could it be?" I laid my pen down on the table and rolled my shoulders.

Bud reached out and placed both hands on my shoulders and rubbed. A deep, penetrating rub was just what I needed. "Your shoulders are full of knots. Relax and let me work them out. Drink water too. That helps release them." Bud instructed.

The more Bud rubbed, the more relaxed I became. I even felt my eyes getting droopy. "We need to get supper. I'm so relaxed I could sleep in this chair. Thanks, Bud." I pushed myself away from the table, stood, and turned to Bud for a hug. I needed one.

We enjoyed a cozy home-cooked meal where we shared the kitchen duties. I made the tossed salads while Bud grilled our salmon steaks. The case never entered our conversation. Bud hinted at marriage, but I didn't jump on the topic. I wasn't ready, so I let it go.

Supper was filling, and once that was behind us, we moved outside. Stars twinkled in the night sky, and the moon was bright as wispy clouds passed over it rapidly. I could feel a shift in the seasons as a light breeze blew through the trees. Shivers ran up my back as I adjusted to the temperature.

We took to our chairs and leaned back, content with each other. I prayed Bud didn't mention marriage again as we enjoyed our downtime. Stars have always held a special place in my heart. Nowhere else could you see them shine than out in the county, away from the city lights.

Bedtime came quickly since arriving home so late. After a quick shower, I slid between cool sheets and laid my head on my pillow. I glanced at my clock as I thought of Taylor and Ivey. I could hear Bud typing on his laptop while my thoughts shifted to Maddox. His smile graced my mind as I realized I hadn't heard from him today.

At 12:25 am, my phone rang and vibrated on the bedside table. I pried my eyes open, willing them to go silent. At the last second, I answered it, and then I bolted upright. "We're on the way." I ended the call and yelled for Bud. "Bud. Hurry. Get dressed."

Bud didn't respond, as he was fast asleep. I thought about leaving him, but he would be so mad. I walked over to the bed and jostled him. He mumbled something, so I did it again. This time, he awoke with a start, and his hand flew to his gun. "Whoa. Bud. It's me. We have to meet Ivey and Taylor. They have a situation."

"I must have been sleepier than I thought. After finishing emails, I laid down intending to get up and change clothes." Bud looked down at the wrinkled clothes and shrugged. "Let's go."

We jumped into my car, and I peeled out of the driveway. After clearing the subdivision, I flipped the control switch for the lights and sirens. There was no sense in waking my neighbors and then having to listen to the wrath.

"What happened, Jada? Are Taylor and Ivey okay?" Bud asked with his eyebrows together.

"They are, but Taylor's informant is dead. That's all I know right now. There's the ambulance." I stated as I pointed.

We pulled into the lot amid the chaos. Taylor leaned against his car with his chin resting on his chest and Ivey rubbing his shoulder. A covered body was lying on the ground off to the left side of the bar. People milled about smoking cigarettes and pointing at the body.

I grimaced when I inspected the scene. Bud did the same. "I'm going to Taylor first. Then I'll look at the body. I don't see Doc James or his group here yet."

Bud glanced at me with worry lines on his forehead. "I'll follow your lead."

We exited the car in unison and headed to Taylor's location. He raised his head when he heard our footsteps on the gravel. "Sheriff. This is bad." Taylor said.

"Tell us what happened, Taylor," I instructed.

"We parked here. Ivey remained in the car when I walked over to the side. We didn't want to spook the informant, so we parked in front. While I stood beside him, a dark-colored SUV drove around the building, and before they passed us, someone in the car opened fire. I think it was a passenger sitting behind the driver. My back was to the vehicle, so I didn't get a look at the shooter, but the vehicle matched Mr. Jurgens's vehicle description. My informant died before he hit the ground. I can't believe I put him in danger, and now he's dead." Taylor reached up to rub his eyes. Then he looked at me for direction. I wasn't sure I could offer anything to soften the blow.

"I'm sorry, Taylor. We certainly didn't want this to happen to him. Somehow, someone found out he had a meeting with you. Let's look at his friends. Do you know who they were? Where did he live? Was there a roommate?"

"He lived with a guy in an apartment on the outskirts of town. That's where I arrested him for the first time. I'll check with him later this morning." Taylor looked at Ivey. "I'm going to the office to write my report."

Ivey looked at me, and I nodded. "Go with him, Ivey. Take him home when he's finished with the report. Or see if you can talk him into going home for a few hours. He can write the report later."

"I'll see what I can do, Sheriff. Talk later." Ivey got behind the steering wheel and pulled out of the parking lot toward the Sheriff's office.

Bud followed me over to the body. Doc James arrived and worked to gather his equipment. We greeted each other, and then he got to work. Using a thermometer, he inserted it into the liver for the body temperature. He confirmed the time of death, just as Taylor had. The victim took one shot from a high-powered gun, inflicting catastrophic damage on the body. The bullet struck center mass and spiraled out from there.

Just as we helped load the victim onto the gurney for Doc James, Deputy Tuttle and Long arrived. "Sheriff. Want us to help with the interviews? Where's Taylor?"

"Ivey drove Taylor back to the Sheriff's Office to start on his report. Although, I had hoped she talked him into going home first. This upset him more than usual. The answer to your question is yes. Thanks for coming over. I heard you worked a car accident. Everything okay?"

Both deputies turn to each other and chuckle. "We arrived to find a fourteen-year-old behind the wheel. He stole his mom's car to get ice cream, and he didn't think to look behind him when he backed up. There was a light pole at the corner of the lot, and now his mom's vehicle had a massive dent in the center of the back bumper and a broken rear window. After we calmed the mother, everything was okay. I feel sorry for the kid when they get home." Tuttle shared the accident scene. Bud chuckled too.

"Well, we all live and learn. Maybe that will be his last time to steal a car. Start your interviews with the people out here. You'll be able to weed through them quickly because they might have seen nothing." I advised. I wanted to look around myself

238

and see if the lot offered any tire tracks. There is only one camera in the bar, and it sits over the cash register. The bar owner doesn't want to invade anyone's privacy by installing outside cameras.

Bud had already begun inspecting the parking lot. His flashlight strobed from one side of the lot to the other as he walked down the vehicle's path. I caught up with him as he bent over, turning over something on the ground. As I got closer, I asked, "what did you find, Bud?" He lifted a gum wrapper in front of my eyes. Then he dropped it in an evidence bag. "It looks too new to have been here long. With so many customers, vehicles would have driven over it before now."

"I agree. It would help us if there were a fingerprint on the wrapper, even though I know Augustus killed that boy. He might not have pulled the trigger, but it involved him or his boys."

Bud continued walking along the road, finding nothing else. We made it to the pool of blood left over from the shooting. I snapped pictures of it now that they had removed the body. The shooter obviously knew about the meeting, but how. Taylor just mentioned it to me this afternoon. Who else did he tell?

"What are you thinking about, Sheriff?" Bud looked at me as he asked me the question. He can always tell when something bugs me.

I turned to face him. "I want to know what I'm missing. An unknown connection lies within this investigation. We need to find it. Someone knew of

239

this meeting, but how did they find out so soon? Taylor just set the meeting earlier in the afternoon."

Bud saw my dilemma. Then he paced while he considered the options. "Who does Taylor's informant know? Friends? Family? Roommates?"

"I asked him those questions before he left. I suggested he make a list outlining those same topics. We can meet him later today to get the list, and then we'll start from there. Somewhere there is an unlikely connection that we haven't seen yet." I added.

After finding nothing else of use, Bud and I climb into the car. I sat behind the wheel and pondered what I had learned tonight. "If Augustus or his guys killed the victim, what's their connection? Was the victim running drugs for Augustus?"

"That's a brilliant question. It makes sense Taylor's informant and Augustus ran in the same circle since both are into the drug business. Has Maddox called you about the warrant on Lyle's phone? It should have arrived by now." Bud questioned.

"I haven't heard from him in several days. The last I heard, he had two agents surveilling Lyle's house. Maybe they're working that angle. Although, I'm not sure how they expect to find Augustus up there when everything seems to happen here." I expressed my curiosity about the lack of intel from Maddox and his US Marshalls. I wondered what they were up to. Glancing at the clock, I thought about calling him, but then I realized it was three in the morning. Bud chuckled when he saw me look at the clock.

"Good choice not to call him at this hour. Let's go home for some more sleep, and then we'll be ready to dig into Taylor's list."

I agreed and pulled out of the bar parking lot. As I pulled onto the road, a dark-colored Tahoe passed me, going in the opposite direction. The driver was unrecognizable. But Bud said, "was that Mr. Jurgens' vehicle?" Without an answer, I flipped the lights and sirens on, turned the car around, and gave chase. It's always been said that some criminals return to their crime scene. Well, I want to know if Augustus did the same. I slipped the mic from its holder and radioed dispatch on my chase. Moments later, Tuttle radioed his pursuit, too.

We traveled on a county back road, weaving across the centerline, making turns with screeching tires, and using a lot of brakes. We glimpsed them one time, but that was it. So, somewhere in this area is a turnoff where a vehicle can hide. This is the area Taylor searched on the satellite.

"Bud, this is the area Taylor used satellite imagery to locate a hiding place. It's still a top priority. They're hiding in there somewhere." I said, defeated. I wiped my brow and placed a loose piece of hair behind my ear. With the mic to my mouth, I radioed dispatch. Our chase ended without a resolution.

I switched the lights and sirens off and watched as Tuttle did the same in his car. We turned around on the road because we would end up in another county if we had followed it. Tuttle turned off in

241

town, and we quietly continued our drive home. Neither spoke as we pondered the latest incident and wondered what would happen next.

Chapter 19

Once we made it home and settled in on the sofa, Bud looked at me. "do you think the drug deal will happen this weekend? Augustus has been on the run for two weeks. If they expect him to be at the drop, I think they would make it happen sooner rather than later. They can't take the chance of us catching him."

"I hadn't thought of that, but that makes sense to me. So, if they set the drug deal for this weekend, we have three days to find Augustus or the drug exchange location, whichever comes first. My gut tells me Micah Sutter knows the exact location, but he won't talk without a deal, and I'm not prepared to offer him a deal after what he did to Aidan and Louisa." I rubbed my neck because this situation wasn't getting better. It's getting worse since someone murdered Taylor's informant right before him. Augustus has brought too many murders to my county.

Bud nodded in agreement. "That takes us back to the pictures. The information is in the pictures. We just haven't found it yet. I'll work on that angle tomorrow." He stood, walked over to me, and kissed me a good night. I watched him stroll down the hallway to the bath, and then I heard his door click shut.

After this case, Bud and I need to discuss our relationship. Do we move forward with marriage? Or do we make better friends than lovers? Maddox stirs something deep within my soul, but is it only a physical attraction? I feel like Bud is my soulmate. He understands me as no one else has—another decision for another day.

I wandered off to bed, still rehashing the same question I've had for two weeks-where is Augustus? When my head touched my pillow, I remembered nothing until morning. I awoke with a start since I had slept so soundly. With five hours of uninterrupted sleep, I felt like a new person. After my shower, I walked to the kitchen, finding Bud already sipping coffee and his face on his computer. "Good morning, Bud."

"Good morning, Jada. I hope you slept well."

"I did. Five hours uninterrupted is amazing." I tilted the creamer and watched as it landed in the bottom of my mug, filling it with steaming hot coffee. I sighed. Leaning against the counter, I took my first sip of the day. The hot liquid slid down my throat with ease. Once I swallow that first sip, I'm ready for the day.

I nibbled a protein bar for breakfast on the way to the office. Ideas bounced around in my head as I worked on a plan of action. "I'm starting with Taylor's incident first, then transition to the pictures. Any ideas?"

There was a moment of silence before Bud responded. "I'll start with the pictures, but if you find something else you need me on, let me know. The warrant for Lyle's phone should be available."

I nodded in agreement as I made a mental note to remember that tidbit. We could ping it and get his location if we had Augustus' phone number from Lyle's phone. "Can you follow up on the warrant this morning? That might prove the connection between Lyle and Augustus."

"You bet," Bud said as we entered the parking lot. I noticed Taylor's vehicle wasn't in the lot. I hope he slept last night. Sleep does a person well, especially when they are hurting.

We entered the side door, and Bud strolled to the conference room as I walked into my office. As soon as I sat in my chair, Maggie appeared in my doorway. "Sheriff. We're being bombarded with media calls on the Augustus case. I'm holding them off the best I can, but I didn't want you blindsided if one slipped through the cracks. Any updates on Augustus?"

"Thanks, Maggie. You know you're the best, right? Never forget it." I shake my head, then continue. "No, no new leads have come forth. I'm sure you heard about the murder of Taylor's informant last night. That was brutal. We're still working on the pictures and waiting for Lyle's phone warrant to come through. Thanks again, Maggie."

She smiled at the accolades, turned, and left. Then I looked in on my desk and found Taylor's report on the top. I read and approved his report. It stated nothing new from our discussion overnight. Behind the report was an extra page containing his informant's known roommates, friends, and family members. The list wasn't lengthy, so I picked up the phone and called for Johnson.

Within seconds, Johnson stood at my desk. "Johnson, I need help with this list. These folks were acquainted with Taylor's informant. During your patrol today, can you and Deputy Long interview these people? We're trying to establish if Augustus and this informant were friends. Someone knew of the meeting last night, and I want to know who knew it and how they found out."

"No problem. Long is waiting in the car for our patrol to begin. If we have no calls, we'll start now." Johnson accepted the list I handed him, and off he went. My eyes returned to the copy I had made of the names. None of the names were familiar to me. I wasn't hoping to garner any helpful information from the list.

Just as Johnson left, Taylor and Ivey entered. Taylor's eyes sported dark circles, and Ivey looked exhausted. "Did you two get any rest last night? If you did, it couldn't have been much."

Taylor answered for both, "we slept a little. I feel better now than I did last night. But this morning, I'm mad. We reread the informant's file, and nothing suggested a relationship with Augustus, Duke, or Jermaine. If there had been, I never would have used him because of the security issue. The file showed the victim working with another drug dealer, but that proves nothing."

"I've asked Johnson and Long to stop in on these people and see what they tell us. We might pick up new leads. Bud is working on the landscape pictures again." My ringing phone interrupted my comments. I glanced at Taylor and Ivey and answered the phone. I listened as Captain Grayson explained Micah requested another meeting with me.

"Well, well. Micah requested another meeting with me. Wonder if he has changed his mind about talking?" I grinned as I prayed for a break in the investigation. I stood from my desk.

"Let us know the outcome. We'll be in the conference room with Bud." Ivey stated.

I walked out of my office and headed to the jail division. I thought about this meeting. Should I give Micah a deal or continue to play hardball? Micah deserves everything he gets in life for what he did to those kids. But I wanted Augustus.

Just as I rounded the last corner, I heard someone behind me yell my name. I turned, and Bud ran to me with papers in his hand. "What's wrong, Bud?"

"I have news that might make your meeting more interesting." He handed me the papers where he had scribbled on them. I had a hard time deciphering their meaning. Then he continued, "Maddox called with the warrant for Lyle's phone. Most of the numbers belonged to a burner phone, but two calls went to Micah Sutter before his arrest."

"That is interesting. Micah knows Lyle, and Lyle knows Augustus. Should we assume Augustus and Micah know each other? Is Micah the one feeding information to Augustus?" I leaned against the wall as I considered this recent information. "We still have Micah's cell phone in evidence. Could we use it to get to Augustus?" I looked at Bud with an eyebrow raised, waiting for his answer.

"We might meet with Micah. Please don't share your knowledge of his ties to Lyle. See what he wants to discuss first. Then, if we have to, we can use his cell phone to set a trap for Augustus."

I nod, thinking about Augustus behind bars once again. This time, his friends, Duke and Jermaine, will join him. The prison system will be less likely to let him leave the prison under the premise of an illness.

Captain Grayson greeted me at the first steel door leading into the jail. I followed Grayson into the jail, and he ushered me into the same interview room where I had met Micah before. I sat in the chair with my arms crossed over my chest and a disgusted look.

A deputy escorted Micah into the interview room and handcuffed him to the bar attached to the table. Micah wasn't going anywhere.

"What do you want?" I said in a not-so-friendly matter.

"We need to talk. I have valuable information for you, but I need protection." Micah pleaded. He didn't have the same cocky attitude as before. Something happened. Maybe someone threatened him.

"Why are you willing to talk to me now? Is someone threatening you?" I asked.

"No threats. I have nothing to lose except my life because of what I did to those kids. I want the others to suffer too. By the way, how was Deputy Taylor's meeting last night?"

That comment felt like a sucker punch to the gut. How did he know about that meeting? I didn't acknowledge the question, but my insides twisted as I sat in that chair. Micah knew he had crossed the line. He recoiled as I stared at him.

"Either tell me what you know, or I'm leaving. You have five seconds." I fumed as I counted down from five, stood from the chair, and called for the deputy. I crossed the threshold and never looked back. Captain Grayson sat at his desk as I sat before him with our eyes locked.

This case frustrates me, but I refused to let it win. "Grayson, how did Micah know about Deputy's meeting? Has he had a visitor or a phone call?"

"I don't recall him having any visitors. He refused to call an attorney because he didn't have money. He signed the paper stating he would use a public defender. I'll check the logs to be sure. Do you want to wait while I check?" He glanced at me with his eyebrows bunched, waiting for my answer.

"No, I'm not waiting. Call me when you have an answer." I exited his office and headed back to the conference room. Maybe Bud and Ivey found something in the pictures.

Bud and Ivey had their heads down with a magnifying glass up to their eyes. They searched for more numbers. "Micah knew about Taylor meeting with his informant. I've asked Grayson to find out how. Micah is square in the middle of this investigation." I said before they knew I was in the room.

Bud and Ivey lifted their heads. "Micah knew about Taylor's meeting. How is that possible? He didn't even call for an attorney." Bud shook his head in disbelief.

Ivey interjected, not mentioning Micah. "I found more words from the pictures. The words are deal, package ready, shipment, I trust. But nothing else. Based on what we have so far, we know there is a shipment on the way, but we don't know when or where the exchange will occur."

I paced the room as I contemplated my next statement. "I want to use Micah's phone. We have it in evidence. I want to know if Augustus' phone number is in his contacts."

"What do you plan to do with the phone? Call the numbers and see who answers. That might create more havoc. Do you think Micah would help us? Could we let him call Augustus from his phone and check the shipment? Or he could let Augustus know we didn't have enough evidence to hold him in jail?" Bud suggested, then he turned to Ivey, who nodded her agreement.

My hands flew to my shoulders as knots formed at the base of my neck and ran across the tops of each shoulder. Pressing down as hard as I could, I received no relief. I paced as I worked through my idea. When I heard a noise, I turned, and Maddox stood in the doorway.

His eyes found mine, and I tried to stave off the sparks, but I couldn't. I don't know why he does me that way. "Maddox. I hope you have something we can use. We're not making headway on the pictures as quickly as we need." I stated as I tried keeping my composure.

Maddox strode into the room. And just his presence creates an awareness like no one else. "I'm sure Bud told you about the warrant. My agents watching Lyle's houses have had only one visitor to the house. It was late in the day, and a flower delivery person. We have photos of the truck and the delivery. A flower shop in Jackson holds the vehicle registration. We're checking on the sender. Lyle goes to work and comes straight home. They even have their groceries delivered."

Ivey asked, "does Lyle know you are on him? Maybe that's why he is careful."

"We don't know for sure, but he hasn't waved to our guys or anything like that. Our surveillance continues. I'm here to discuss Lyle's phone." Maddox looked at me as he said it.

"That's what we were discussing. We found out that Micah Sutter, the street car racer, is involved somehow with Lyle, and now we assume he knows Augustus. Micah sits in our jail, and his name appears on Lyle's phone. If we have Micah and his cellphone, we want him to help us find Augustus." I laid out my idea, hoping the group would approve.

Maddox had a time following my train of thought. "Let me work through this. Micah was the guy who presumably killed Aidan, and he dragged the girl down the road, leaving her for dead. His number showed up in Lyle's contacts on his phone. Micah is in your jail, and you have his cellphone in evidence. Is that correct?"

"Pretty much. We also have copies of the landscape pictures Augustus drew and gave his visitors. We found a code hidden in the pictures, but it takes a long time to decipher each one. Maybe using Micah will give us the information we need quicker." I shared my thoughts, but I wasn't sure I agreed with my own idea when I said it aloud.

Bud saw my confusion. He spoke up, saying, "your plan could work if Micah agrees to it. Do you trust him enough to follow through with the plan?"

All eyes turned to me. I stammered because I wasn't sure how to answer Bud's question. "I'm not sure. Micah has toyed with me from the moment we arrested him. He knew we were searching for Augustus and offered nothing. Now that he knows he is being charged with murder, he wants to talk. Why? What does he expect to get from me?"

Everyone in the room shrugged their shoulders. "He might be after leniency. This could be a way to keep him off death row." Maddox offered.

As I continued pacing, Maddox studied a few of the pictures. Bud answered a call, and Ivey stepped away for coffee. Maddox walked over to me and said, "how are you, Sheriff? I never checked on you after your injury."

"I'm okay. Just frustrated over this case. I want Augustus off the streets, and we're so close to seeing that happen." I looked at Maddox, and my heart quivered. He saw it too.

My cellphone rang deep in my pocket. When I plucked it out, I answered Captain Grayson's call. Maddox watched me as I listened to Grayson give me the details of Micah's information dump. I nodded my head, and I ended the call.

As everyone returned to the room, I shared the recent information from Grayson. "Another inmate received a visitor. It turns out this visitor is a friend of Micah's. The visitor shared the details of Deputy Taylor's meeting with his informant to another inmate, and that inmate told Micah. That's how he knew when I met with him. Can I assume Micah knew Taylor's informant?"

"It sounds plausible to me, Sheriff," Ivey stated.

Then Maddox asked, "what are these numbers signifying?" Maddox pointed to the random list of numbers we garnered from a picture. "Phone numbers?"

"That remains to be seen. They don't seem to correlate with our code, so we're still considering possibilities." Ivey answered for us.

I called Grayson and set up a meeting with Micah in twenty minutes. It's now or never. We need his help, and waiting around won't answer our questions. Everyone's eyes rested on mine when I ended the call. "What? There's no sense sitting around, wondering if he'll help us. I may as well ask him." I waved at the group as I said, "I'm going to my office for a few minutes. Then I'll let you know what he says."

On my walk to my office, I stopped at the coffee bar since I had just enough time to enjoy a cup before I met Micah. As I lifted the cup from the counter, I felt a presence behind me. I suspected the reason. When I glanced up, Maddox stared back at me.

"I wondered if I was ever going to get you alone," Maddox stated sternly.

"Want a cup? There's plenty." I tried to make light of the subject, but he stepped into my space, and as he reached for a cup, his arm brushed against mine. I stopped because I couldn't bring myself to move.

He poured coffee into his cup and took a sip. "This is great coffee. What kind is it?"

"I order it online. It's a special blend my dad introduced me to. I can't give it up." I turned my eyes down because I didn't want to share my sadness with Maddox.

"I'm sorry I asked. Some memories are painful. I wanted to tell you I'm sorry for putting you in an awkward situation. You and Bud are together, and I would never come between you. Just know you can count on me if the need arises. Any time of day or night." Maddox rubbed my arm, then turned and left.

That exchange certainly caught me by surprise. At least Maddox gave me the answer I needed. He won't pursue me because of Bud. For that, I'm thankful. But when I checked the clock on the wall, I realized I was late for my meeting with Micah. So, I tilted my cup to my lips for the last sip of coffee and trotted to the jail division. Captain Grayson waited at the counter for me.

Chapter 20

"Grayson." I greeted him, but my insides were a mess after my discussion with Maddox. With only a few minutes until I meet Micah, I must refocus on my reasons for seeing him. This conversation is a make or break for this case.

I followed Grayson into the same bleak interview room as before. The same cold chair sat waiting for me. As I sat, the door opened, and in shuffled Micah. The first thing I noticed was his unkempt hair and his sunken eyes. I couldn't tell if he just rolled out of bed or what, but he looked rough.

"Micah. I'm here because we need your help." I watched his eyes shift, and he contemplated the meaning of my statement. He didn't respond, so I continued. "We know you and Lyle Fins are associates because your phone number was on Lyle's phone. We want you to help us find Augustus."

Waiting during the break was hard. I wanted to say everything and discuss it, but Micah's mental state led me to question my intent. He wasn't fidgety today, and his eyes remained focused on the table. What could have happened to him?

I leaned into him. "Micah, talk to me. What's going on?"

He said nothing for a second. Then I saw a flash in his eyes. "I can't call Lyle or set them up. I would be dead in twenty-four hours, even in here. Can you protect me? I don't see how. Augustus has people inside these walls too. I'm surprised I'm still living."

"Give me the names of Augustus' people. I'll see you remain separated from them. If you won't make the call, what do you know about the drug deal? We know Augustus escaped because Lyle needed him outside for a massive drug deal to happen. Anything you can tell me will be helpful."

"Sheriff, what happens to me when you transfer me to prison? You can't watch my back in there. I'd rather die here than go to prison and have to look over my shoulder all the time." Micah's head drooped as his chin fell.

How can you make someone who feels helpless understand the importance of the knowledge he holds? "Micah, I can't say that I understand your feelings because I don't. I've never experienced being on the other side of the bars, but I can tell you if you share whatever information you have on the drug deal, you can help save hundreds of people. For that, I'll talk to the judge." After explaining my position, I stopped talking and leaned back against the cold metal chair. Micah needed time to process the information.

Two minutes later, he whispered, "Saturday night. The deal goes down Saturday night at midnight."

I breathed a sigh of relief. At least I have a date. "Where?"

Micah shook his head from side to side. "I don't remember ever hearing the location. It will happen in your county, Sheriff. Augustus is here too."

"Do you have a phone number for Augustus?" I wanted to cross my fingers, hoping for the number, but I knew that wouldn't help.

"He changes burner phones daily. Augustus always said to trust no one but him." Micah shook his head and realized how stupid it was to follow Augustus. Money was Micah's driving factor in joining Augustus, and now it's his downfall.

"One more item, Micah. We found out how you knew of Deputy Taylor's meeting. Is the inmate that passed you the information about Taylor's meeting one of Augustus' guys? Why did he share that information with you?" I asked, then waited. I wanted the answer to the second question.

"Yes, he is a part of Augustus' network, and they told me to prove they can get to me, even in jail. Do you know how Augustus found out?" Micah questioned.

"Our assumption is the informant let it slip to someone, and they notified Augustus or one of his guys. Am I close?"

Micah nodded in agreement. Having nothing else to ask, I stood. I'm walking away with the date and time of the exchange, but the location remains unknown. I glanced back at Micah as I walked through the door. With his demeanor deflated, he never looked up. He sits with his shoulders slumped and his eyes fixated on the tabletop.

Grayson met me on the other side of the door. I didn't know what to say, so I said nothing. I simply waved at him as I passed. Micah is one of those people that can't handle the thought of being locked in a cell for the rest of his life. I'm another. I don't think I could survive anything like that mentally. He doesn't have a family in Georgia, so his family visits would be slim to none.

I stopped at the coffee bar because I needed to refuel. Then I continued to the conference room. Bud, Ivey, and Taylor were hard at work. All heads turned my way as I entered. They studied my face before Bud asked, "What happened with your meeting?"

With my energy zapped, I sat and sipped my coffee before starting. Over the next several minutes, I rehashed Micah's conversation. I described Micah's state of mind and his appearance. Ivey put her hands to her mouth as it shocked her. When I stated the date and time of the drug deal, the group perked up, waiting for the next tidbit. But once I shared, I had no idea of the location. Their shoulders drooped in defeat.

Taylor stated, "Micah offered the time and day, but he claims he doesn't know where it is happening. That seems odd."

I nodded, showing agreement with Taylor's statement. "Micah was in a strange state today. I'm unsure if another inmate threatened him or he accepted we would lock him away for life. The cocky attitude is gone, and he looks pathetic. I want to change our concentration. Taylor, have you found anything on the satellite imagery maps? If this exchange takes place this weekend, it won't happen in town. It will be secluded."

"I'm still looking at the area along the river. We know Augustus likes the river, but we have miles of riverbank to search." Taylor explained as he pointed to his laptop showing the satellite maps.

Without having a follow-up, I sipped coffee and pondered my meeting. In a way, I felt like Micah held back on information. He stayed fixated on the table, but I wonder if he used that tactic to keep me from looking in the eye. I've never seen someone's demeanor change one hundred and eight percent over a day.

Bud and Ivey studied another picture. Ivey jotted something on her paper. I didn't even ask about it. I walked out of the room and headed to the bathroom. Alone time is what I need more than anything. I brushed my hair, splashed cold water on my face, and walked to my office.

The radio sounded as I sat in my chair. I listened to dispatch as they toned for an ambulance to the high school soccer field. I grimaced. That call could be something as simple as a sprained ankle. No one knows until they reach the scene.

Bud entered my office a little while later and walked over behind me, placing his hands on my shoulders. He began rubbing the knots that had formed again. "Micah's meeting was difficult. I can tell. Do you know what caused the change in Micah? Something or someone took the air out of his balloon."

"Not really. Grayson proved the inmate shared Taylor's meeting with Micah. Micah seemed to think they shared that information to prove Augustus could reach him, even in jail. I wonder if Micah didn't tell all he knows."

"Well, Sheriff, you need to visit Micah one more time. This will be Micah's last chance at redemption." Bud suggested. "Or do you think he will talk to someone else?"

I lifted my eyes to Bud's. "Who do you suggest?"

Bud shrugged his shoulders, "Taylor." Then he paused. "It would shock Micah to see Taylor after asking about his meeting. Taylor was also there for Louisa. It might be a worthwhile interview."

Considering Bud's suggestion, the more I thought about it, the more I liked it. "I like it, Bud. Will you come with me to discuss this with Taylor? Taylor must promise to keep his temper in check before I agree. If he traumatizes Micah, we'll lose our case for Aidan and Louisa, and I can't let that happen." I emphasized I'm not willing to force information from Micah, but we must capture Augustus pronto. We have too many open murders in this county that involve Augustus. He can't slip away without punishment.

Bud and I returned to the conference room. Taylor's head was leaning over to his laptop. "Taylor, did you find something?" I ask, eager to hear the reply.

"I thought I did, but I guess not. Nothing showed when I enlarged the area, but there appears to be a minor blip on the map." Taylor shook his head. His body language proved this process is frustrating him.

"Taylor, Bud, and I have a question for you. If you feel uncomfortable, you need to speak up." I stated, while looking at Taylor.

"Ok. Sure. What is it?" Taylor piped up, and Ivey rolled her chair over too.

I lifted my hand to Bud, showing him to start the conversation. "Sheriff and I were talking about Micah and the change he took. We think he knows more than what he gave us. We would like you to talk with Micah about us. Maybe he will open up with a man, and you were there for Louisa." Bud paused and waited. Taylor was deep in thought as Bud spoke.

Then I added, "but you must keep your temper in check when you meet. We can't take the chance of ruining our case against Micah."

Taylor nodded, then said, "I want to take a crack at Micah. I understand about my temper. When can I talk to him?"

"I'll make the arrangements with Grayson." I walked out of the office, dialing Captain Grayson with my phone to my ear.

Grayson agreed to Micah's interview with Taylor. He said Micah would be in the interview room in fifteen minutes, and he warned me Micah hadn't changed since my interview. Micah has withdrawn by sitting on his cot all day. He stopped reading books too.

I shared Grayson's information with the group, which didn't deter Taylor from the meeting. Taylor paced the room, locked his phone and gun in his locker, and made his way to the jail division. He possessed nervous energy, and he knew he needed to calm it. He didn't want to come across so intense or forceful that Micah refused to talk.

Grayson met Taylor at the door and escorted him to the interview room. Someone had already seated Micah at the table. Micah's disheveled appearance surprised Taylor, but he pushed it into the back of his brain. He had other things to discuss.

Micah's eyes shifted around the room as he tried not to look at Taylor. Surprise showed on Micah's face as he realized Sheriff Steele wasn't meeting him. Taylor greeted him, and Micah responded.

Taylor got down to business as he explained his reasons for meeting him. Micah nodded but didn't respond. Continuing their talk, Taylor expressed their urgency with having only two days remaining until the drug deal. Micah fidgeted in his chair when he heard Taylor's voice, stressing urgency. Taylor questioned Micah's knowledge, and Taylor witnessed a flash of recognition in Micah's eyes.

They volley back and forth for a while about Augustus, Aidan, and Louisa, then they return to the current topic of the drug deal and finding Augustus. Micah wore down after an hour or more in the room, and he finally divulged fresh information. They set the deal for a location on the river at a hunting cabin. They didn't give him an address. Supposedly, the hunting cabin is merely four walls, without water or electricity to the place.

After a while, Taylor grew weary when he had no further questions, and he felt Micah had told him everything. Micah understood he had no reason to withhold information since they charged him with murder. He has no bargaining chips left.

Taylor returned to the conference room to find Bud and Maddox working on the landscape pictures. Sheriff Steele and Ivey stepped out for coffee. Taylor sat in a chair and waited for the ladies to return.

Once everyone rejoined the group, Taylor shared his experience with Micah. Then he dropped the bombshell about the hunting cabin on the river. Excitement grew as everyone felt the shift.

"Does Augustus or his family own any land at the river? Or maybe Duke or Jermaine?" I asked as I thought about the river. "Actually, they probably don't own it. It's a cabin they found, or a friend told them about it. They don't want us to trace it that way."

Neither Bud nor Maddox commented on the information. Both turned their heads to the numbers on the whiteboard. "What are you thinking? Both of you are on to something."

Bud looked at Maddox, and in unison, they stated, "GPS coordinates."

"What?" Ivey asked with a strange expression on her face.

Maddox explained, "those unexplained numbers might be GPS coordinates for the drug deal location."

Then Bud followed, "Taylor, can you plug in the numbers and see if they return to a cabin on the river?"

"Absolutely. Let me log in, and then I'll be ready." Taylor tapped the keys on his laptop, and once his screen appeared, he said, "ready."

The first couple of tries didn't pan out. After they finagled the numbers, the third and fourth tries placed a star in the ocean. But the fifth try hit pay dirt. It was the same area Taylor worked in this morning. It shows a blip on the map but zooming in distorts it, vanishing.

Everyone fist-bumped their neighbor when they had the missing piece to their puzzle. Now, to put us all together. They had the location, time, and date of the drug deal, but how did they handle the takedown?

"This cabin is in the middle of nowhere. It appears to be surrounded by trees, with the river fifty yards away on the northwest side. I'm unsure of a road that would get us to the location. We need someone that knows that area." I expressed my concern about the terrain.

Maddox suggested a coordinated takedown with all three departments, US Marshalls, FBI, and my department. I liked the idea of having the resources available. US Marshalls and our department would arrest Augustus, while the FBI would handle the drug deal. If it turned out to be as much as Micah suggested, it would look good on a stat sheet.

Maddox and Bud jumped on their phones, working out the arrangements. Bud came back with more resources. "Our drone operator will send a drone to do a flyover for additional topography. If the trees are thick, it might not help, but we need to try since we are walking in blind."

"That's a brilliant idea. Did they give you a time frame for when this was happening?"

"We should have an answer by tomorrow at noon. Then we can complete our strategy and be ready for the takedown." Bud explained.

I looked over at Taylor. "Taylor, you did a magnificent job with Micah. Thank you for speaking with him. I know that was hard for you."

"It was difficult, Sheriff. But I'm glad I did it. Thanks for trusting me." Taylor added.

"I'll notify the deputies to keep Saturday free because we have a trip to the woods that night." I stepped away from the room, the happiest I had felt in a while. Now, if I could make it until Saturday night and see Augustus captured, everything can get back to normal around here.

As I passed Maggie's desk, I heard her with a press member on the phone. She repeatedly made her statement. I walked over and asked for the phone. She passed it to me. I introduced myself, then I listened.

Once the reports had their say, I had mine. They weren't happy when I ended the conversation, but they understood why we must keep things a secret. I advised once everything was over, I'd have a news conference. I placed the phone on the cradle, and Maggie uttered "thanks" under her breath.

"Maggie, are you getting many press calls?"

"All day, Sheriff. It's like they know something is happening in the county, but they're unsure what is happening. It's driving them crazy. The reporters call here to see if I'll slip and share something important." Maggie shared.

"It will only be one more day of this. Things are moving along for us. I don't want to tell you the specifics yet, but rest assured, Augustus will wear handcuffs in a few days." I smiled as I meant what I said. I walked off. Then I remembered why I was going to my office. "Maggie, can you call Tuttle, Long, and Johnson for me? I need them in my office ASAP. If they're not available, I'll catch them up later."

"Sure, Sheriff, right away." As I turned around to leave, Maggie already had the phone in her hands.

While Maggie contacted the guys, I studied the board again even though I shouldn't have to. Since I've seen it so much, it should be embedded in my brain. But I wanted to make sure we overlooked nothing. If they set the drug deal for Saturday, the buyer is local or staying at a nearby hotel. With a local buyer, why would they need Augustus? My bet is the buyer is from out of town. So, where is Lyle in all this? Maddox hasn't mentioned him.

Chapter 21

Maggie interrupted my thoughts by stating, "only one of three guys was available."

"Ok, Maggie. I'll put the meeting off until shift change, so I only have to state my business once." I turned my attention back to my thoughts.

Bud entered with papers in his hand. "The drone results are disappointing. Here are the pictures from the drone flyover. The trees are too dense to capture much about the cabin. Although, the drone found a secondary road that we could use to get us closer to the cabin. This road will put us about a quarter-mile from the cabin."

I took the pictures from Bud and glanced at them. The secondary road was barely visible. It would make our efforts less if we could use it. "I like the idea of the second road. Another concern that no one has approached is booby traps. We can't forget what Augustus and his guys did to the US Marshalls. No matter the direction, it will be a slow march to the cabin."

"We must remind everyone of that incident. Everyone involved in the takedown must be on guard for booby traps." Bud stated as he jotted a note for himself.

Bud and I discussed several plans for the takedown. We laid out plans if we came in from the second road, the main road, or walked through the woods. If we walked in through the woods, we felt sure we would encounter booby traps. Almost like they would expect it. If Augustus knows this cabin, then more than likely, he'll be familiar with the second road. That leads us to believe it will be booby-trapped, which leaves us no straightforward way to reach the cabin.

We struggled to decide on a plan. Before I knew it, my deputies arrived at my door. "Hey, guys, come in and take a seat. Bud and I are planning for the takedown. Saturday night, Augustus' drug deal takes place. We'll be there to capture Augustus, his guys, and the drug buyer. There will be a group from our department, the FBI, and the US Marshalls taking part in the takedown." I watched as each head bobs. "Do you want to be part of the takedown team?"

It was a resounding yes from each man. Then I continued, "I want to point out the dangers." Once I stated the obvious, Bud and I tag-teamed on the drone maps and what Taylor found on the satellite imagery. The last bit of information we mentioned was the potential booby traps.

None of my men backed down. They were ready to find Augustus above all else. If they arrested the drug buyer, that's a plus. I explained I hadn't spoken with Long yet, but I planned to have him on road patrol Saturday. I wasn't ready to let Long take place in this takedown since he was still a rookie. His time will come.

I advised the team we would meet at the Sheriff's Office tomorrow afternoon to complete the plan, then they would have a few hours of downtime before reconvening for the trip to the cabin. I watched each man exit my office with a determined look. Even though they knew the dangers, they still opted to join the team.

As I prepared to leave for the day, my desk phone rang. I reached to grab it before it switched to voicemail. Doc James called. I waved my hands to get Bud's attention. "Doc James, Bud is here with me. Give me a second to put the phone on speaker." Bud walked back to his seat while I pushed the button for the speaker.

"Ok. Doc. Tell us what is so important." I stated.

Doc James shared the news of the DNA test from Aidan's murder scene. "Blood matches Micah, and several fibers found on Aidan's jeans match Micah's car upholstery. Also, we found a gun registered by Micah at an Alabama address that matches the same caliber that killed Aidan. We got him, Sheriff."

"You were right, Doc. This is fabulous news. I'll add murder to his growing list of charges. Thanks, Doc. Have a good evening." I ended the call and turned to Bud.

"Doc James made my day. I know Taylor will be happy, too." I found a clean piece of paper on my pad, and in red ink, I wrote myself a reminder to handle the additional charges for Micah. Now, if the takedown goes as planned, everything will fall into place.

Bud and I left the office hand in hand. We planned a nice, quiet, home-cooked dinner, and I couldn't wait to start. Today boasted abundant sunshine, and the night would follow without rain, which sent us outdoors. We loved our backyard with the fire pit and the grill. It's a perfect way to wind down. Since it's so hot during the summer, we don't use it often, but we make it come alive when the time is right.

The next day, we drove to the office early. I wanted to make sure everything we needed was available. Maddox was already standing in the conference when I entered. Bud, Maddox, and I rehashed the plan many times, making changes, then finally agreeing on it. The FBI and the US Marshalls had ten-person teams traveling to help with this today. Now, I feel ready to tackle the job.

While we waited for the groups to arrive, I made copies of the maps we used to set the plan. As we prepared to enter an unknown area, maps helped save lives. Since the woods are dense in this area, the team must know avenues of escape if something catastrophic occurs.

As I finished with the last stack of maps, I heard a commotion in the lobby. All eyes turned to me. Bud followed as I headed to the lobby to handle the intrusion. When we turn the corner, I hear, "There he is. Bud, we're here!" I chuckled.

The FBI team arrived in fashion. They brought tons of equipment on carts, and the wheels crossing the threshold made a screeching noise. I blamed the activity on Bud. A few of the people entering the building I've met before. They were here for the serial killer case. We shook hands, and I showed them to various areas of the Sheriff's Office. Most asked for the bathroom and coffee.

Maddox found us in the lobby and added his team was pulling into the parking lot. We have another group of ten. Two of the ten are the agents who suffered gruesome leg injuries. Their doctor cleared them for duty. After their incident, they're eager to be a part of the takedown team.

"I'll wait here for my team. Show the FBI team to the conference room." Maddox suggested to me. I followed his suggestion.

With so many in the room, I scrounged up chairs and other necessities. Then I asked Maggie for pots of coffee. I didn't foresee spending too much time in the room, but these people traveled to get here, and some might need coffee.

The FBI group opened cases upon cases of material and laptops. They set aside the ear mics for our use. This will keep all team members on the same channel instead of having their own communication outfit. Emotions welled up in my soul as I realized that this would not be possible without Bud.

Minutes passed before the US Marshalls team strode into the room. The size of the team astonished me. This team is all about muscle mass. Maddox whispered in my ear, "this team is the elite takedown team of the US Marshalls. We got this,

Sheriff." Then he squeezed my hand. I cringed because the hand squeeze was unexpected. He winked as he stepped away.

We settled into the room, and I began the meeting with introductions. Then Bud, Maddox, and I shared points to the plan. Each member sat at the table with a packet of information. We asked them to study the terrain and the plan over the next several hours. The team will leave the Sheriff's Office at 10:00 pm. We wanted to be situated before ten in case the buyer showed early.

No one asked questions, so we ended the meeting. I slid out of the room because Deputy Long texted me and asked me to meet him in my office. So, I did. He stood erect with his hands behind his back. "Deputy. What can I do for you?" I asked him.

"I want to be a part of this takedown. While I'm fresh out of the academy, I'm ready." Deputy Long stated. Then he waited as I processed his request.

"While I'm happy with your enthusiasm, I can't in good conscience send you to this takedown. You'll be the point of contact for the Sheriff's Office tonight. I need you here to be ready for anything. If anything drastic happens, you're our lifeline."

"Sheriff, I understand, and I'll be here for you and the rest of the teams." Deputy Long appeared gloomy for a second until I asked him to remain here. He felt like we needed him, and we did.

We brought in pizza and soft drinks for the evening meal, then Maggie returned with homemade chocolate cookies. The team consumed them in record time. Maggie grinned as she catered to everyone's needs.

At 9:45 pm, we met once more to prepare for our deployment. We placed our mics in our ears and did a radio check with the tech guy. Bud gave us a pep talk, and we loaded into our vehicles for the twenty-five-minute drive. The second road appeared without difficulty, and we turned onto it without headlights. We were lucky the moon afforded us ample light to see, as the road was a narrow dirt road.

We sat in our vehicles for a few minutes, waiting, listening, and watching. If someone spotted us, we would know soon enough. Bud squeezed my hand before exiting the truck. Then I flashed back to Maddox. I prayed for everyone's safety before my boot touched the ground.

The enormity of the situation came into focus when I rounded the truck. Twenty-six people were preparing to walk in harm's way. Long and Ivey were in my ear, giving me a calm feeling.

The teams took their role, the snipers moved into position, and we began the slow trek to the cabin. Each member carried a compass, but we had to use the ones for darkness. Since we didn't want to be a beacon for Augustus, we used blackout bags. It was slow going as we often stopped to check our location. The terrain was such that we couldn't walk a straight line.

By 11:00 pm, the teams and snipers were in place. We waited, listened, and watched the area for movement. We didn't know if Augustus used security patrols or thought this location was secure. The only thing I saw was mosquitos. Big ones, the kind you see fly in front of your face. I'm glad we had the forethought to spray for bugs before leaving.

At 12:05 am, Maddox's voice breaks the radio silence. "A single SUV approaches the house with an unknown number of occupants. Two were visible in the front seat. The vehicle has Florida tags. Acknowledge."

Every team member acknowledged Maddox's intel. We readied for the inevitable fight. There was no way Augustus would go down quickly, and everyone knew it. The buyer pulled alongside the front walk and exited the vehicle, leaving a guy standing next to it while another led him into the cabin.

We won't approach until the exchange has taken place. Fifteen minutes pass before the front door opens. Augustus and the buyer exit the cabin. They shake hands, then part ways. While Augustus and his guys walk to his vehicle, the buyer does the same. Our time was now.

Maddox yells from the cover of darkness for the subjects to drop to their knees, place their hands over their heads, and interlock their fingers. That didn't happen. Chaos ensued as the team members rushed to the vehicles and attempted to subdue the felons. Gunshots cut through the night air, striking trees and kicking up debris. Ivey spoke through the ear comms, requesting a status report. No one replied.

Augustus ran from the vehicle. I yelled for him to stop. He paused, turned around, locked eyes with me, then bolted. Taylor followed Augustus, forcing him into Maddox's path, but Augustus was unaware Maddox hid in the shrubs. Maddox greeted Augustus with a gunshot to the thigh. Maddox stepped out of the woods and ran to Augustus. He removed the gun from Augustus' right hand, and as he reached for handcuffs, Maddox froze.

Duke jabbed his muzzle into Maddox's temple hard enough to knock him off balance. He yelled, "let Augustus go, or I will kill you." Duke never flinched as he stated it over and over. Augustus continued squirming on the ground from the gunshot wound while blood trickled down his pants leg. Duke stared at the other officers, but he never wavered.

Taylor stopped short when Duke appeared. He hid behind a large oak tree while Bud and I scrambled to save Maddox. We whispered to the other team members to secure the buyers and Jermaine before joining the hostage situation.

Tuttle found a spot next to Taylor after he helped secure Augustus' vehicle. They wouldn't be driving out of here tonight. Bud and I spoke with Duke and described Augustus' injury in detail. We told Duke Augustus would die without medical attention. His stance never changed. Duke pushed the gun muzzle further into Maddox's temple.

I knew in my heart I would never let Augustus leave these woods unless he was in a body bag or handcuffs. Maddox locked eyes with me. He never gave me the impression of being afraid. If anything, he was more determined to see this through.

Bud whispered in my ear, "Sheriff. Concentrate on Duke, not Maddox. Duke will show you signs. If he tenses, that's your sign of moving."

Deputy Johnson and one each of the FBI and US Marshalls team sat at the ready with their sniper rifles. If Augustus passed out, we would end the saga by authorizing our snipers to end Duke's life. That is no decision anyone wants to make, but sometimes it is a must.

Minutes ticked by when, finally, each sniper acknowledged their location and asked if they had a clear shot of Duke. The US Marshall had a clear line. I approached Duke first with my hands out at my sides, showing I wasn't carrying a firearm. "Duke. Let's discuss your situation. You know we won't let you leave. Please put the gun down before someone else gets hurt." I waited as I watched Duke process the information. Duke's eyes roved the scene. He searched for an escape plan. When he realized his chances were slim, his hand tightened on the pistol, agitated. I stepped back into the darkness, and Bud stepped out.

He spoke with Duke, but Duke never responded to him. Duke asked for me. "Sheriff, can you guarantee our safety in jail?" He asked as he looked at Augustus lying motionless on the ground.

"I'll do my best, Duke. Augustus needs your help. Now, put the gun down." I watched his eyes twitch. Then they grew to mere slits. His jaw worked as his cheeks moved. Is he going to shoot Maddox first? I screamed at Maddox. He ducked, and a sniper pulled the trigger, striking Duke. Duke never knew what hit him.

Jermaine wailed in the back seat of our car as he watched his friend lose his life. I called for an ambulance and a patrol escort to the hospital. Deputy Long obliged. We would remain on the scene for a while since the state police received notice of our shooting and were en route. While waiting, we scoured the cabin, putting our pieces together, and found many items of interest.

Augustus and his friends hid in the cabin, which is why no one spotted them in town. We found items belonging to Hazel and Mr. Jurgens in the cabin linking Augustus to the murders. We had our case if Augustus survived. For our efforts, we arrested one of Miami's most prominent drug dealers and Lyle Fins, for his involvement. My county would again be in the spotlight when the trial began.

After three hours with the state police, they cleared us to leave the scene. We returned to the office for a debriefing. Maddox took center stage as he thanked everyone for their participation. He commended his sniper for taking the kill shot and saving his life in front of the group. The sniper never looked away from Maddox and only gave the group a slight nod.

We released the teams to pack their gear and head home. While they packed, I watched Maddox interact with his group. It was effortless, and his team supported him one hundred percent. I left the room as I tried to separate myself from Maddox. There was no use dwelling on past decisions.

As I passed the coffee bar, I stopped and poured a small cup. With the time of night, I probably won't sleep anyway, so why not sip on something that calms me? Maddox sidled up to me and reached in for a hug. "Thank you, Sheriff. You saved my life. I'll never forget it. If you ever need anything, you know who to call." Then he turned and walked away without a glance back.

Books by Series

MacKenzie 'Mac' Morris
MOA Book 1

Flames of Murder Book 2

Wage of Murder Book 3

Digger Collins
Pieces of Murder Book 1

Murder for Justice Book 2

Murder by Testimony Book 3

Sheriff Jada Steele
Promises of Murder Book 1

Murder Cove Book 2

Detective Ryker Bartley
Mission: Murder Book 1

Detective Clint Rugbee
Murder at Beachside Book 1

Waves of Murder Book 2

About the author:

A.M. Holloway is an author of murder, mystery, crime, and suspense books with a dash of romance for added excitement. She was born and raised in Georgia and still lives in the northwest part of the state. When not writing, you will find her with family enjoying the outdoors or sitting in her favorite chair daydreaming about her next book.

Visit **www.amholloway.com** for new releases and

to sign up for my reader's list or simply scan the code.

Also follow me on:

Facebook @amhollowaybooks

Instagram @amhollowaybooks

Made in the USA
Monee, IL
26 February 2023